CAPE MAY HYDRANGEAS

CLAUDIA VANCE

CHAPTER ONE

It was a bright and sunny mid-May morning, and Dave and Margaret were about to go to their third open house tour of the day in Cape May. Dave parked the truck on a side street, and they walked up to the dilapidated-looking house on the corner. A large dumpster full to the brim sat on the street, and the house's yard looked like it hadn't been maintained in years. All the overgrowth made it look like a jungle.

Dave looked at the home's listing on his phone as they stood outside. "Well, I see why the realtor didn't post interior photos online. Looks like this is definitely a fixer-upper."

Margaret walked in first, noticing a handful of other couples were already inside the house looking around. She observed the crumbling stairs to the second floor, then glanced at the floors, feeling slightly optimistic. "Well, it has hardwood floors. That's a plus."

A woman came up to them after finishing talking to another couple. "Hi! I'm Danielle. I'm the realtor doing the open house. Take a look around and let me know if you have any questions."

"Perfect. Thanks, Danielle," Margaret said as she moved to the other side of the room.

Dave cleared his throat. "I've got a question. This house is being sold as is? Is that correct?"

Danielle nodded. "That's correct."

Dave sighed as he followed Margaret.

Margaret stepped into the dining room and looked up. "Well, there isn't a ceiling in the dining room. It's just beams."

Dave shook his head in dismay as he walked towards the kitchen, or what was left of it. "Come see this in here, Margaret."

Margaret walked into the kitchen and glanced around the room with confusion. "There's only a single sink in here. What's that about?"

Dave shrugged. "I don't know, but I'm not loving this house. I don't mind a fixer-upper, but this is out of my league. And I don't like that it's being sold as is."

Margaret looked out the window. "You ready to leave?"

Dave took one last look around and nodded. "Yep."

As they headed back towards the front door, Danielle stopped them. "So, what did you think?"

Dave glanced at Margaret. "It's not for us."

Margaret sighed as she looked at the hole in the living room ceiling. "It's just not what we're looking for. I'm sure the right person will come along and make this place fabulous."

Danielle smiled. "I'm sure too. We've already got three offers today alone."

Dave's eyes widened in shock. "Are you serious?"

Danielle nodded. "Yep. I think it's the location; it's such a great neighborhood. What are you two looking for?"

Margaret chimed in. "Something with lots of land. We love to garden and farm."

Danielle laughed. "Well, why did you come look at this house? The yard is pretty average sized."

Dave shrugged. "We're just trying to explore all our options, I guess. We've been house hunting since April, and we're starting to realize it's not as easy to find that perfect-for-us-home as we'd hoped. I feel like we've looked at a ton of houses at this point."

Danielle reached into her pocket and pulled out a business card, then handed it to Margaret. "Here's my card. I can try and help you find that dream home. Send me an email with your requirements and information, and I'll see what I can come up with."

"Thanks, will do," Margaret said as she stepped out of the house with Dave behind her.

They got to Dave's truck, but before opening the door, Dave patted the top of the truck's roof. "You hungry? Because I am. How about we go get something to eat?"

"You read my mind," Margaret said as she hopped into the truck.

Dave got in, started the engine, and glanced over at Margaret. "Where to?"

Margaret thought for a moment. "How about Beach Plum Farm?"

"Sounds good," Dave said as he shifted into drive.

Ten minutes later, they were pulling onto Beach Plum Farm's gravel driveway and parking.

Margaret got out of the truck, then turned around to face the farm market and smiled. "See all those green bushes along the front there? Those are hydrangeas. By next month, they should be blooming. It makes my heart so happy when they bloom."

Dave smiled. "Agreed. We'll have to come back and see them in action," he said as he walked towards the market door, but not before stopping to smell the potted rosemary on the bench.

They walked through the beautiful rustic building and back outside to where the kitchen window was. There, they looked at the menu, ordered, then found a shady picnic table among the raised bed gardens.

Not long after, someone brought their food out. Margaret

got a cucumber cream cheese sandwich and Dave ordered roasted vegetables over grits. It paired nicely with their iced tea.

Dave took a bite of his grits, then glanced around at the lush, gorgeous property. "A person could get pretty inspired being here."

Margaret smiled and nodded as she watched some chickens roam around. "I'm always inspired here."

Dave sighed as he scanned the raised beds. "I'm just thinking about all the houses we've looked at over the last few weeks. None of them were big properties. I mean, yeah, there was that one place, but the house was more in shambles than the one we saw today."

Margaret nodded as she took a bite of her sandwich. "And then there was that one house that was absolutely stunning but had the smallest yard ever. I've seen bigger yards in the city," she said half-sarcastically.

Dave shook his head. "At this rate, I don't know when we're going to find a house that suits us."

Margaret reached into her pocket and pulled out Danielle's card. "You know what, I'm going to email Danielle now. Might as well. Maybe she can help," Margaret said as she took out her phone and started typing.

Dave shrugged. "Can't hurt, I guess. By the way, what's going on with your cousin Audrey? She still wants to buy your house?"

Margaret sighed. "I think it's a go. I spoke with Audrey yesterday. They're pretty excited about it. Rob already found a job near here, and Audrey has some interviews. They'll need to move in by mid-June. I'm so worried that we won't find a house by then."

Dave took his last bite of the roasted vegetables and took a long sip of his iced tea. "This is starting to get more stressful with all of these deadlines."

Margaret forced a smile. "You're telling me. I was so

excited about getting a garden started in the new place, but I've got to get stuff in the ground no later than mid-June, and even that is pushing it. Plus, with all the moving and making the new house ours, will there be time?"

Dave rested his hand on Margaret's across the picnic table. "There's a lot of what ifs here. I'm hoping that everything will work out somehow, but who knows. I've already got the beach house rented out all summer except for Fourth of July week, and one other week that I can't remember. I figured if your family is coming again, we'll need it."

"Thank you," Margaret said as she got up to take their empty plates to the dirty dish tub by the trash cans. "Why don't we stop at Liz and Greg's before we go to the last open house?"

Dave stood up, and they headed towards the parking lot holding hands, but not before Margaret realized that she hadn't fed the chickens yet.

"Have any quarters?" she asked excitedly.

Dave reached into his pocket and pulled out two. "Feeding the chickens, eh?"

"Yes," Margaret said as she walked over to the chicken feed vending machine and stuck the quarters in, letting the pellets slide into her hand.

Dave laughed as all the chickens in the area hurried over to Margaret when she crouched down and let them peck at her hands to get to the food. "Doesn't that hurt?"

Margaret shrugged. "Not really. Once in a while, you get a sharp beak in there, but mostly they're gentle."

Dave stooped down to try and pet a chicken, but it quickly ran away. "I guess they want no part of me," he said with a chuckle.

Margaret finished feeding the birds and stood up. "Did you want to walk the property and see the pigs and fields? I think the hives are back there too."

"Sure," Dave said as he grabbed Margaret's hand while they headed up the gravel driveway.

After some walking, Margaret stopped as she caught a glimpse of the beehives off in the distance. "Look. There they are. I find beekeeping so fascinating. It's amazing the things you can do with lots of land."

Dave nodded as he looked towards the pigs who were happily sleeping. "Looks like the pigs are enjoying the nice day."

Margaret chuckled. "They are adorable. It feels so good to be out here feeling the sun on our skin, taking in nature."

"It's our happy place. We love being outside," Dave said as he gazed off into the distance in thought.

Margaret looked back towards the path they'd walked up "Hey. I just got an idea. Let's stop at Duckie's Farm Market and get a key lime pie to bring to Liz and Greg's. I think they'd love that."

"Sounds good," Dave said as they walked together back to the truck and headed out towards Duckie's.

After picking up a key lime pie and leaving, they found themselves making their way up the long driveway to Liz and Greg's.

They stepped out of the truck to hear Greg's voice coming from the backyard. "Come around back!"

Dave glanced at Margaret. "Did you tell them we were coming?"

Margaret shook her head. "Nope. I forgot. I figured we'd just drop in."

They walked around towards the backyard to find Greg turning over the soil in one of the gardens with a shovel. He stopped to wipe the sweat off his forehead with a bandana in his pocket before waving at Dave and Margaret.

"Hey, Greg. What are you up to out here?" Dave asked as he looked at the freshly cleaned and turned garden plots, feeling thoroughly impressed.

Greg sighed as he looked over all the work he had done, feeling satisfied. "Well, I think we're just about done getting the garden ready for planting. Pulled up all the weeds, added compost, and leveled it out."

Just then, Liz appeared from behind the garage in dirty rolled-up pants, a baseball cap, and garden clogs. "Hey, guys!"

Dave chuckled. "Who knew you two were gardeners deep down?"

Liz looked down at her garden clogs and laughed. "Well, I don't think deep down we were. I suspect you two imprinted it on Greg. I still haven't gotten the hang of this, honestly. Oh, did you stop at Duckie's?" Liz asked as she saw what Margaret was holding.

Margaret handed her the pie box. "We sure did. Thought you guys would enjoy this."

Greg's eyes lit up. "I'm eating a heaping slice of that when I get inside. Thank you."

Liz took the pie inside to quickly drop it off before coming back out. "What do you guys think of what Greg did? Does it look alright?"

Margaret smiled. "It looks great. You're doing a fantastic job," she said as she longingly glanced at the garden patch where her tomato plants used to grow.

Liz followed her gaze. "Are you sure you don't want to plant stuff here this year? There's plenty of room. Greg doesn't plan on using those two big plots in the back, and I'm sure you can till up some new plots."

Margaret sighed and thought it over while glancing at Dave. "No, I think we're going to hold off. We're still looking at houses, and—"

"Oh, that's right. How's it going?" Greg asked.

Dave shrugged. "It's going, but it's not easy. It's a seller's market and everyone is putting in offers well above asking. City folk are coming out here in droves, paying cash for properties. It's hard to compete with that."

Margaret nodded. "Not only that, but the options are slim pickings. Today we looked at an extremely rundown place, and the realtor told us it already had multiple offers. A few years ago, that house would have been on the market for months."

Liz frowned. "Can you just stay put until the market is better or until you can find something you love?"

Dave glanced at Margaret. "Well, our place in North Cape May is booked with summer rentals, and Audrey, Rob, and their kids already have plans to move in in June. We can't cancel on them. Rob has a job lined up, and frankly, we're excited to have them come to Cape May. Everyone is really."

Liz bit her lip. "Oh, that's right. How could I forget?"

Margaret watched some birds fly by. "Our dream is to find a nice big property to have our own garden and farm on, but at this point, I'm not getting my hopes up. I would love to still have time to get a garden in wherever we buy, even if it's small one."

Dave nodded. "We're going to keep on looking. We have a couple houses to see tomorrow. Keep your fingers crossed."

Margaret changed the subject. "Greg, I'm excited for you to have a garden for the restaurant. You can't get any fresher than that."

Greg lit up. "You know, I'm pretty excited about it myself. My staff is also loving the idea. They plan to help out with maintaining the gardens and harvesting produce. In fact, a few of them should be arriving in about an hour."

Dave smiled. "Can't get any better than farm to table. What are you planning on growing?"

Greg looked at his one of the freshly hoed plots and sighed. "Well, heirloom tomatoes in that row, zucchini there, lots of peppers, eggplant, lots of herbs, and plenty of cucumbers. I'm sure we'll add more things as we go. I have to say that this just makes running a restaurant all the more special. We're going to be growing a lot of the food that we're serving to our guests at Heirloom. It's going to be something."

"I can't wait to try what you cook up. It's going to be incredible," Dave said happily.

Liz held up her hand. "And I somehow got roped into helping with the garden against my will," she said half-jokingly while staring at Greg. "On another note, I'm going to keep my eyes peeled for houses that are for sale for you guys. We need to find your Cape May dream property. I just know it's out there waiting for you."

CHAPTER TWO

Chris ran the hose from the dock to his pontoon birding boat to wash off the deck and inside floors. The sun shone extra bright on his red shoulders while everyone else with boats at the dock did the same. It was officially boating season, and the birding tours were in full force.

Brewster the cat came out of the store, walked up the dock, stood five feet behind Chris, and let out a meow.

Chris lowered his sunglasses and looked behind him. "Brewster, buddy! You loving this nice weather?"

Brewster chirped and rolled over, belly up, letting the sun warm him.

Chris laughed. "I'd pet that belly of yours, but I gotta finish hosing the boat down."

A car pulled into the parking lot, and out stepped Sarah. She caught Chris's eye and waved.

"Hey, you. What are you doing here?" Chris asked as he continued hosing the boat off.

Sarah walked towards Chris and stopped to pet Brewster, who was now fast asleep in the hot sun. "I don't know. I was kind of bored, and I thought I'd come visit."

Chris chuckled. "Bored, eh?"

Sarah stood up and sighed. "Yeah. My managers at the coffee shop are incredible. I hate to say it, but they're running that place better than me. Sales have been up since they've been on board. I stopped over for a half hour today, but there really wasn't much for me to do. Tonight, I'll put in stock orders and review finances and payroll, but that won't take long. I guess I need to find something to do," she said as she watched another boat pull into the dock.

Just then, a gorgeous tall college-aged blonde girl with a crop top and cutoff shorts walked out of the dock shop. "Hey, Chris, a customer is on the phone. He wants to know if you rent life jackets?"

Chris nodded. "We do, Natalie. You'll see the price list on the wall behind the register."

Natalie smiled at Chris and then at Sarah. "OK, great. Thanks!" she said as she walked back into the shop.

Sarah crinkled her nose. "Who is Natalie?"

Chris knotted the hose and walked up to the dock to turn it off. "She's my new hire. We needed someone to work in the shop while I'm giving birding boat tours. It's Ralph's daughter —he runs the dolphin tours. She's in college and home for the summer, so it worked out nicely. I guess I forgot to tell you."

Sarah bit her lip, a little apprehension sneaked in about Chris working with such a stunning young girl, but she hid it. "Well, OK, then. Whatever works."

Chris kneeled down to pick up Brewster and cradled him like a baby as he stroked his fur. "So, you're looking for something to do, eh?"

Sarah stumbled on her words. "Well, um, not exactly. I'm sure I can find—"

Chris cut her off. "Why don't you work the birding tours with me? You can help spot birds and educate everyone. We can tag team."

Sarah scratched her chin in thought. "Really? You think I'd be good at that?"

Chris smiled. "I sure do. You're good with people. A lot better than me, actually. Plus, you'll enjoy being out on the water, and of course, we'll get to be together."

Sarah reached over to stroke Brewster, who purred away in Chris's arms. "That sounds easy enough. That's all you'll need me to do?"

Chris thought for a moment. "Well, I'm sure I could use help here and there on the dock, as well, if you wouldn't mind."

Just then, some paddleboarders went by, laughing and enjoying the day. Then, some kayakers passed, looking peaceful and happy.

Sarah smiled and took a deep breath of the fresh sunny air. "You know, I think I would really enjoy this. I'm down. When do you want me to start?"

Chris let Brewster jump out of his arms, then put his arm around Sarah's shoulder and kissed her on the cheek. "This is so exciting. I can't wait to work together. How about this weekend? The first birding boat goes out at 10 a.m. on Saturday. Just be here by nine thirty. Does that work?"

"I think so. If I need to stop at Monarch, I'll go beforehand. OK, well I'm going to the store. I'll see you when you get home," Sarah said as she leaned over to kiss Chris.

Chris waved goodbye as he walked back towards the boat to clean the inside windows with a rag and spray.

As Sarah got to her car, she was stopped by a sound. She looked over to see Natalie walking out of the shop talking on her cell phone. She headed onto the dock and leaned over the railing, giggling and flipping her long blonde hair back over her shoulder.

Sarah looked down at what she wore: khaki capri pants and a workout tank top with beat-up sneakers. Her hair was in a tight bun, and she was pretty sure her chin had broken out in pimples since she tried a new night serum the other night. It had been way too long since she took care of her gray roots. Suddenly, she didn't feel attractive in the least.

* * *

That afternoon, Dale drove with Donna to South Broadway Avenue and parked. He stepped out of the car to get Donna's door.

"OK, don't open your eyes yet," Dale said as he carefully led her out of the car.

"What are you showing me, Dale?" Donna asked as she latched onto his arm.

"You'll see," Dale said as he led them in front of the building. "OK, you can open them."

Donna popped her eyes open. "Why are we at Grandmother's Gravy?"

Dale smiled. "Well, they closed, and I bought the space. It's going to be my new restaurant's location."

Donna's eyes widened. "Are you serious? They accepted your offer?"

"Yes, can you believe it?" Dale said as he put the key in the door and opened it.

They walked inside of what used to be the old Italian restaurant. It had dingy carpeting and still had tables and chairs inside. It looked untouched since it was last open.

"What are you going to do with all of this? Keep it here?" Donna asked looking at everything that was left behind.

Dale shook his head. "No way. This is not my restaurant's aesthetic at all. This will all come out and be donated or trashed. A dumpster arrives tomorrow as well as a construction crew for the renovation. I want this place up and running by the end of June."

"Wow. You move fast," Donna said as she looked at a vase full of dusty silk flowers on the host stand. "What's your vision for this place?"

Dale walked to the other side of the room, then turned around to face Donna. "I'm so excited—there're beautiful hardwood floors under this carpet, so those will be refinished. There's going to be an open kitchen like at Porridge in Collingswood. I'll put in a nice big bar over there and get custom-made farm style tables and chairs for the dining space. It'll actually be a farm market and restaurant in one. I'm thinking big garage-door style windows that roll up when the weather's nice—right here instead of these walls. There's so much more, but I don't want to give everything away just yet."

Donna tried to contain her excitement. "Oh, wow. I can't wait to see it. You really think it'll be done in time?"

Dale nodded. "I do. The guy I hired to work on it did Porridge's construction. He's got the best crew around, and he's quick. I've never seen anyone work more efficiently than Joe. I just have to get to work on logistics and getting a staff in here. It's going to be very busy."

They walked out of the restaurant and back to the car, where Donna stopped in her tracks when she caught a glimpse of Greg's restaurant, Heirloom, three doors down. "Oh, my gosh. I totally forgot that Grandmother's was on the corner of the street that Greg's restaurant's on. You're going to be so close to him. How cool is that?"

Dale opened the car door and got in. "Yeah, about that ... I haven't told him yet."

"What? Why?" Donna asked, surprised.

Dale sighed. "I'm afraid of what he'll say. I feel like I'm imposing on his space. You know, possibly taking away customers from him. I don't know. I'm just worried about how he'll react."

Donna put on her seat belt and stared straight ahead at

Heirloom. "Oh. Well, if you're worried about that, why did you buy this place then?"

Dale put the car into drive. "Because it was the best option for my restaurant, and I needed to find something. It was this place or a rundown store across town. It was a no-brainer."

* * *

Dave and Margaret stood next to a very busy road and stared at a house across from them.

Margret squinted her eyes to get a better look as cars and large trucks *whooshed* by behind them. "Where did you find this house?"

Dave thought for a moment. "I saw it online last night."

Margaret sighed and rolled her eyes. "Well, I guess we can go look at it. I'm not too thrilled with the location, though."

Dave shrugged. "Agreed. I didn't realize this is where it was located before we arrived. Sorry about that."

Margaret glanced at the driveway, noticing six cars were parked. "What's with all the cars? Lots of people looking at the house today?"

Dave shrugged. "I'm guessing so. Though, I already don't see the appeal."

As they walked to the front door, a large truck zoomed by and leaned on its horn, startling both of them.

Dave stopped just as they got to the door. "I think a realtor is supposed to meet us here, but we're early. Fifteen minutes early to be exact. I guess we should wait."

Just then, the door popped wide open, and a jovial guy held out his arms, as lots of people and kids hung out inside eating food, laughing, and talking. "Hey, there! You guys here to look at the house?"

Dave stumbled on his words. "Well, um … yes, but we're waiting for the realtor."

The guy waved his hand. "You don't have to wait. We'll

give you the grand tour. This is our home. We're actually having a family reunion today. The wife organized it months ago, but I need this house sold. So, we're killing two birds with one stone, ya know?"

Margaret's eyes widened as she looked over at Dave. "We can come back another time."

"Oh, nonsense. Don't let my loud family scare you off," the guy said with a chuckle as he ushered them inside.

He stopped at the living room. "Well, here's the living room."

The entire room of family all waved their hands. "Hello there! Wanna a bite to eat?" one of the relatives asked from the couch.

Margaret forced an awkward smile. "No, we're good. Thank you."

The guy looked back at Dave and Margaret. "Where are my manners. I'm Hank. Over there in the kitchen is my wife, Gretchen."

Dave took his hand out of his pocket and waved to Gretchen. "Nice to meet you."

Margaret smiled while waving, feeling more than ready to get out of the house.

Hank pointed to a back room. "Now, follow me this way. The house has three bedrooms and wait until you see what I did with the third."

Margaret looked at Dave, trying to signal that she wanted out. Dave sighed and nodded, not sure how to rush the process since they already knew they didn't want the house.

Hank led them to a bedroom and swung the door open. "Voilà!" he said as he opened his arms wide to show off his collection of taxidermy animals all over the shelves and walls.

Margaret felt her stomach turn. "Oh … interesting."

Just then, they heard a woman loudly talking in the hallway about houses.

Dave scratched his chin and looked out into the hallway. "Is that our realtor?"

The realtor stood talking with another couple and glanced over at Dave. "Are you Dave?"

"That's me," Dave said with a half-smile.

"I'm so sorry I was running late. I have another couple here to see the house. I hope you don't mind," the realtor said as she glanced around.

Margaret popped out of the dead animal room next to Dave. "We don't mind at all. In fact, I think we've seen enough. We're going to be heading out. Thank you, Hank," Margaret said as she grabbed Dave's arm and headed towards the front door.

Once outside and back in Dave's truck, Margaret and Dave gave a sigh of relief. "I've never been happier to be back in this truck," Margaret said as she slunk down into the seat.

Dave nodded, put the truck in drive, then looked over at Margaret. "Dare I ask if you want to look at the second house I found online? Another realtor is supposed to show us the place in twenty minutes."

Margaret stared back at Dave, not sure of what she wanted to do.

Dave shrugged. "Look, I can cancel. It's not a big deal."

Margaret looked at her watch, then out the window. "No, let's do it. We're not going to find anything by not looking."

Fifteen minutes later, Dave pulled up and parked in front of the house. A realtor sign sat in the front yard, and by all accounts, this home looked very normal compared to the last one. No cars in the driveway, and it was in a quiet neighborhood.

Margaret smiled as she stepped out of the truck. "This place is cute, though anything would look cute compared to that last place."

Just then, the realtor pulled into the driveway and got out while talking on her phone. She nodded at Dave and Margaret and held her finger up, signaling to give her a minute, as she unlocked the front door.

"OK, Derek. Noon tomorrow sounds good. I know you're going to love this place in Avalon. It's right on the beach," the realtor said as she disconnected the call and put her phone in her purse. "Hi, I'm Chloe. You're Dave and Margaret, correct?"

Margaret smiled and nodded. "That's us," she said as they followed Chloe inside the house.

Dave and Margaret looked around the house when they stepped in. It was newly renovated and seemed very nice and ... normal."

Margaret gave a long sigh of relief. "This place is cute. So far, I like it."

Dave walked over to the refrigerator and opened it. "Wow, this is a nice fridge. Clean as ever, too."

Chloe pointed to the other side of the house. "This house has four bedrooms and two bathrooms, if you want to follow me this way to take a look."

"Perfect," Margaret said as she clapped her hands.

After ten minutes of looking around, they stood in the living room together when Dave remembered something. "We still haven't seen the basement yet. Is there one here?"

Chloe fumbled on her words. "Oh ... that's right. There is one. It's nothing special, which is probably why I forgot about it. Follow me this way."

They walked down the creaky wooden steps into the basement, noticing shelves and shelves filled with storage bins packed full of items. For the most part, it was a typical unfinished basement, nothing special, like Chloe said.

Dave walked around the area one last time before noticing a door off to the side. He opened the door, flicked on the bright fluorescent lights to see a very old dusty dentist exam chair in the middle of the room. Along the sides of the room were old rusted dental tools and hundreds of teeth molds and dentures, which appeared to be real.

Margaret walked in beside Dave and held a hand over her mouth. "What in the world?"

Chloe sighed as she peered inside. "The owner used to be a dentist back in his heyday many years ago. I guess he did home appointments? He never got rid of this stuff."

Dave's stomach turned. He hated the dentist, and there was nothing creepier he could find in a house.

They made their way back upstairs where Chloe looked at her watch. "Well, I've got to get going in a minute to show another house. What did you think?"

Just then, a man opened the front door and peered inside. "Hi! It's Ben from next door. Just making sure the place wasn't getting robbed," he said with a chuckle.

Chloe folded her arms. "Nope, I'm the realtor showing the home for them."

Ben walked inside and took a look around. "Well, that's good. It's easy to see why the Mitchell's are ready to move."

Chloe squinted at Ben, obviously annoyed. "Why's that?"

Ben cleared his throat. "Oh, you know, warmer weather down south … and to get away from the ghosts. Well, I'd best be going," Ben said as he headed for the front door.

Margaret's eyes widened as she looked over at Dave. He was still processing what he'd seen in the basement, and now this just landed on him.

Ben abruptly turned back around. "Well, I hope that didn't affect your buying decision. I probably shouldn't have opened my mouth," he said as he left, heading back to his house next door.

Chloe shook her head as Margaret and Dave followed her outside and she locked the front door behind them. "Probably," she muttered.

Dave and Margaret got back into the truck, this time with Dave feeling immense relief to get out of *that* house.

"So, what did you—" Margaret said before Dave cut her off.

"Nope. That's a big hard nope," Dave said as he put the truck into drive, practically peeling out of there. "It might be fun to stay at a haunted bed-and-breakfast, but I don't want to live in a haunted house if I don't have to."

CHAPTER THREE

Judy and Bob stood together talking at the back of the Cape May Movie Theater, when a couple walked up to them and showed them their tickets.

Judy took out her little flashlight, shone it on the tickets, and looked straight ahead. "Follow me. Your seats are this way," she happily said as she walked ten rows down the aisle.

Bob then ushered another couple a few rows past where Judy had just gone. They met at the back of theater again where Bob put his hand on Judy's shoulder. "So, are you enjoying volunteering here?"

Judy nodded. "I'm loving it, aren't you? It's so fun to connect and talk with people from all walks of life. Plus, we get to stay for the movie if we want. You can't beat it."

Bob chuckled. "The staying for the movie part is great ... if I can stay awake for it."

Judy playfully nudged him, then watched as a huge crowd of moviegoers approached them from the lobby. "Well, we've got our work cut out for us. The past few times we've been here, there's been a packed, sold-out crowd. It's so wonderful to see this theater thriving."

Bob nodded. "It is. Now, if only we could revive the drive-in theaters from when we were kids. I miss them."

A couple standing next to Bob overheard him. "Did you say drive-in theater? You know there's one about an hour from here, right? Great place with great food. We take the kids about once a month. It's worth the drive," the man said.

Bob's eyes widened. "You're kidding? How did we not know about this?"

The man smiled. "It's called Wesley's Drive-in. It feels nostalgic to me, and I didn't even have them growing up. I think you two should go check it out."

Judy smiled as she looked at the couple's tickets and walked them down the aisle to their seats. "We definitely will."

After another twenty minutes of ushering people to their seats, they finally found two seats in the very back of the theater next to each other to plop into for the movie.

Bob put his arm around Judy as the red curtains on the stage opened to reveal the large movie screen. The popcorn machine worked overtime in the lobby, and the smell of its buttery, salty scent wafted into the theater.

Judy turned to Bob and smiled. "How about Sunday?"

Bob shifted his eyes. "What about it?"

"For the drive-in, assuming they're open. Let's go check it out then," Judy said.

Bob's eyes lit up. "Really? You're down for that?"

"Of course. If the weather is nice, let's do it," Judy said as she smiled and turned back to the screen just as the previews started.

Bob's heart leapt ten times as he remembered the last time he'd gone to a drive-in movie theater—it had been many years. "Maybe I can dust off the old Impala in the garage, and we can take it there."

Judy nodded. "That might be nice since we only take it out for Sunday drives these days."

The movie finally came on, but Bob's mind had drifted

elsewhere as he envisioned what a drive-in theater would look like in this day and age.

* * *

Margaret, Dave, and the girls walked into Lucky Bones for dinner that evening.

After getting seated by the host, they all looked over the menus as they ordered their drinks.

Abby and Harper pushed their menus to the end of the table, then took out their books to read.

"Did you two decide what you wanted to eat already?" Margaret asked surprised.

Harper looked up from her book. "Yep. We're sharing a pizza."

Abby didn't move her eyes from her book.

Dave chuckled. "When did you two become such bookworms?"

Harper put her book down and rolled her eyes. "We've always read books, silly."

Dave laughed. "Well, true, but not at restaurants. This is a new thing."

Abby finally looked over her book at Dave and Margaret. "Well, they just solved a huge mystery in my book, and I didn't want to stop reading before we left."

Harper nodded as she picked her book back up. "And I have to read a chapter by Monday for class. We're going to discuss it, and I want to get it over with."

Margaret smiled. "Well, this is great. I love to see you two reading."

They ordered, the food came, and the girls ate with one hand while reading with the other. It was quite comical.

Noticing the girls weren't paying attention, Margaret felt comfortable bringing up the house search. She hadn't wanted to talk about it in front of the girls yet, so as not to upset them.

They didn't know about the whole moving plan yet, and Margaret didn't want to bring it up until things were finalized.

Margaret took a bite of her Caesar salad, then glanced at Dave who was enjoying his burger. "So, I checked, and I haven't seen any new listings in Cape May for us to look at."

Dave nodded, while finishing his bite. "After yesterday, I'm scared to even look for a while."

Margaret sighed. "I hear you. I'm starting to wonder if we put the cart before the horse by making that agreement with Audrey and Rob before we found another place," she said trying to sound vague so the girls wouldn't understand what they were talking about.

Dave shrugged. "Maybe. I guess I never realized how many places *aren't* for us."

Margaret heard a chirp, which signaled an email notification on her phone. She looked at it and said, "Talk about timing, look who just emailed me," then held the cell phone's screen towards Dave.

Dave squinted to get a better look. "Danielle? The realtor from the open house tour the other day?"

Margaret nodded as she opened the email to read it. "That's the one. I wonder what she wrote." After a minute, Margaret put her phone down, and started eating her Caesar salad again.

Dave stopped eating his burger and looked over at Margaret. "Well? Anything?"

Margaret smiled. "She has a place for us to check out tomorrow. It's actually not even listed yet, so we'll be seeing it early. She thinks it might be perfect for us."

Dave chuckled, picking up his burger again. "Well, I'm kind of scared what someone else's version of perfect is ... because that man's taxidermy room was his definition of perfection."

Margaret shrugged while laughing. "Well, I did email her our requirements like she asked. Hopefully, she went by that."

Dave finished his burger and wiped his mouth with his napkin before taking a sip of his drink. "Well, I'll be working tomorrow, but how about I take a long lunch break and we'll head over?"

"Sounds perfect," Margaret said still feeling skeptical but also optimistic at the same time.

They paid the bill and headed out of the restaurant and back to the car, and the girls kept reading as they walked.

Dave tousled their hair playfully. "OK, now this is going overboard. You're not looking where you're walking. Someone's going to trip."

Harper was about to disagree when she nearly dove headfirst into the gravel parking lot after tripping on a cement parking block, but Dave caught her just in time. Harper's heart raced as she clung to Dave's arms. "Well, you're probably right about that," she said as she started laughing.

Margaret laughed along with her. "OK, no more reading until we get home. Let's focus on getting to the car."

* * *

Liz was busy working from home with her interior design business when Greg called from the restaurant.

"Hey, Greg," Liz said as she sorted through a stack of papers on her desk.

Music and loud kitchen noises could be heard behind Greg. He yelled into the phone, "Hey. Liz?! Can I ask a favor?"

Liz looked at the work in front of her. "Well, I'm—"

"Can you go out and water the garden for me? I totally forgot to before work, and the seedlings we just planted are going to dry out with this warm sun today," Greg cut in, still yelling into the phone over the noise of the kitchen.

Liz sighed and shut her laptop. "Sure. I guess I could use a break."

"Perfect! Thanks, Liz. I gotta go. We're super busy right now," Greg said.

"Got it. Bye," Liz said as she walked towards the back door.

Outside, she turned the hose on and sprayed the newly planted garden with the sun hitting her face, and it felt wonderful. The air smelled fresh, and she could hear lots of songbirds. She took a deep breath and savored the serene moment.

She was snapped out of her blissful state when a swarm of bugs appeared in front of her face. She held the hose in one hand and tried to swat them away with other, except it didn't do much. The little gnats flew into her eyes and nose, so she ran with the hose to the other side of the garden, where she was finally away from them. Liz took a deep breath, this time feeling relief to be away from that ordeal.

The feeling, however, was short lived when she noticed water on her shoes and looked down to find the hose leaking. She turned the nozzle off in order to examine where the leak was coming from. When she tightened the nozzle, water started spraying right into her face, blinding her.

"Ahhh!" Liz screamed as she felt her way around the garden while rubbing her eyes.

Suddenly, she stepped right into a mud puddle in the garden, probably from all of the excess water. She looked down to see the cute expensive flats that she'd thrown on to quickly water the garden now completely soiled.

She heard a noise and glanced over to see one of the boys had let the dogs out the back door. Both dogs barreled towards Liz, tromping all over the muddy garden before jumping on her out of excitement. Now her clothes were wet and covered in dirt.

"Greg!!!" she yelled out to nobody in frustration. "Seriously?!"

She turned the hose off at the spigot and hobbled inside,

making sure to take off her shoes before she stepped in the house.

Michael and Steven were on the couch watching TV and turned around to look at their mother. "What happened to you?" Steven asked.

Liz rolled her eyes. "I got attacked by a hose, bugs, and some excited dogs at the same time."

Michael chuckled. "Should we not have let the dogs out?"

Liz laughed. "Well, you didn't know. It is what it is. I'm going to go wash up."

She walked into the bathroom and stared in the mirror, feeling thoroughly annoyed. Suddenly, she was ready to hang up her gardening clogs for good.

* * *

Dale walked around his restaurant as the construction crew busily worked on the new place. He held up a couple of paint swatches to the wall, trying to pick out the perfect color.

Joe, the general contractor, walked over to Dale. "I like that gray swatch. Has a clean modern look, and it isn't too dark or too light."

Dale nodded. "I was thinking the same exact thing. I'm probably going to go with that. How's everything going so far? Is it more work than you thought?"

Joe looked back at the kitchen where demolition by the crew was in full swing. "Actually, not at all. Structurally, it's solid. I'm pretty positive we'll have this place ready for you by mid-June."

Dale's eyes widened. "Really? I'm so glad to hear that. Thank you."

"No problem," Joe said as he headed back to the kitchen.

Just then, the front door opened, and in walked Donna, holding a bag.

"Hey, you," Dale said as he gave her a hug.

Donna handed him the bag. "I made you lunch. I know you're going to be here all day. This place is moving along quickly," she said with a sigh as she looked around.

"You made me lunch?" Dale said, his heart growing two sizes.

Donna blushed. "Well, I figured you'd need it."

Dale put the bag down and grabbed her hand. "Come. Let me show you what they're doing."

They walked back to the kitchen to see some walls knocked out. It didn't look like much yet except for a big mess.

Dale crossed his arms and smiled as he took it all in. "This kitchen is going to be completely new and modern. It's going to be amazing, and it's going to be open like the one in Porridge. Guests like to see their meals being made—and frankly, I like it too."

Donna smiled at the idea of Dale running a super successful restaurant in Cape May. "It's going to be amazing."

They walked out of the kitchen and into the dining area.

"Well, I'd better be going," Donna said.

"What are you up to today?" Dale asked.

"Classes are over for summer break, and school's not in session, so I can't substitute teach. I'm trying to figure out what I can do for work. I'm going to try and revive my clothing reselling business, I guess. Maybe hit up a couple thrift stores on the way home from here?" Donna said.

Dale paused for a moment. "I have an idea for a job for you."

Donna furrowed her brow. "What's that?"

"The funnel cake cart. Memorial Day weekend is in a week, and that's when busy season starts. Honestly, I wasn't even going to do it this year with how crazy everything is with opening the restaurant, but maybe you would like to do it," Dale said as he scratched his head in thought.

Donna shook her head. "I don't know, Dale. Being cooped

up behind a funnel cake stand all day? I think I'd be miserable."

Dale shrugged. "Look, we can go fifty-fifty on profits. I'll pay for all the overhead costs, and you don't have to work every day. You can hire people out. Heck, maybe the employees I had last summer want to come back. You could make some phone calls."

Donna thought for a moment. "Fifty-fifty, huh? That sounds pretty good. That would work for you?"

"Definitely. I'll still make a small profit, you'll have a means to make money, and you'll be right there on the Wildwood Boardwalk by the ocean. The location can't be beat."

Donna smiled as she opened the front door. "I guess I could give that a try, but I'm telling you, I know I'm going to hate it."

Dale gave her a kiss as they walked outside together. "Well, think about it, and let me know."

CHAPTER FOUR

Margaret and Dave drove down a back road in West Cape May bordered by corn fields, horse farms, and eventually a forested area full of lush green overgrowth.

Margaret's eyes widened as she rolled her window down. "How have I lived here all these years and never been down this way?"

Dave shrugged as he slowed the truck a little to find the house number they were looking for. "Well, I think because this road always seemed like private property. It has a dead end, and it's off the beaten path, that's for sure. It's not like it's on the way to anywhere."

Margaret rolled down her window as she squinted to see the numbers on the mailboxes by the street. "One twenty. There it is. I think that's it."

Dave steered the truck onto the gravel driveway. As they slowly drove up the long winding path, the smell of lilacs wafted through the open windows. Margaret let her head hang out of the truck and took a deep breath, savoring the sunny fresh-floral-scented breeze.

They made it to the house and parked right outside of it. Margaret stepped out of the truck with Dave and did a three-sixty scan of the area. "There are acres and acres of land here. Farther than the eye can see. Is it part of the property?"

Dave looked off into the distance to watch a blue heron fly high before landing behind the tree line. "Well, I sure hope so."

Margaret turned her attention to the withering old yellow farmhouse that stood in front of them. "I guess this is the house …"

Just then, another car drove up the driveway and parked next to them. Out stepped Danielle, the realtor. "Hey, guys. Sorry, I'm running a bit late. I was showing another house across town. Are you ready for the tour?"

Margaret nodded excitedly. "More than ever."

"Perfect," Danielle said as she walked up the front steps onto the big wraparound porch. She put the key into the front door lock and turned, but before opening it, she glanced at Margaret and Dave. "Did I tell you two the history on this house yet? I can't remember."

Dave shook his head.

Danielle took a deep breath. "Well, the couple, Mr. and Mrs. Lewis, lived here for around fifty years. The house was built in the 1930s sometime. You'll see that when we go inside. It's very old, and as they got older, it became harder and harder to maintain. They are both in their late eighties now, so to make things easier, they moved in with their daughter in Florida. It worked out rather nicely, and the kids are helping them sell the place."

Margaret felt her heart sink a little. A house that hadn't been maintained in a while sounded similar to some of the awful places they'd already looked at. She glanced at Dave, who nodded and smiled at her.

"OK, let's head inside. Watch your step," Danielle said as she opened the front door.

Margaret and Dave stepped over the threshold into a very old empty house with widened eyes.

Dave fixated on a large fireplace in the living room, then on the hardwood floors throughout the space. "Well, this sure has a farmhouse feel."

Danielle nodded. "It does. They weren't farmers, but the wife loved to garden and paint. She would spend entire days out in the yard doing watercolor paintings of her beautiful flowers."

Margaret smiled as she walked towards a bright sunroom that sat off the dining room. "Wow. Look at this."

Danielle smiled. "That's where she kept her plants. I'm told she adored that room. She was always in there."

Dave walked next to Margaret and put his arm around her back. "It's stunning. You don't see rooms like this very often anymore."

"Exactly. It's why old homes are so unique. They hold so much character. Wait until you see the kitchen. I think it's my favorite room in the house," Danielle said excitedly.

They followed Danielle into the space and were met with exposed brick on the walls, large wood beams lining the ceiling, and black-and-white checkered tile on the floor. Sunlight poured throughout the room from the many large windows, and above the countertops were wooden shelves.

Dave rubbed his hands together and leaned on the center island with a vintage chandelier hanging above and stared towards the long white farmhouse sink. "I see why this is your favorite room. I'm in love with it."

Margaret put her hand over her heart. "So am I."

Danielle smiled and pointed to the ceiling. "Want to take a look at the bedrooms? There're four."

"Yes!" Margaret blurted out.

Dave laughed as he followed them upstairs.

Danielle opened the door to the far back room first. "This is the main bedroom. It gets a lot of sunlight, and the view out the window to the backyard is something."

Dave stood at the window and gazed out. "The property is gorgeous. Is all this land theirs?

Danielle nodded. "It is. They bought their neighbor's property behind them twenty years ago."

Margaret looked out the window, feeling her heart flutter. "Can we go look outside now?"

"Well, sure. We can do that," Danielle said as she headed down the stairs and to the back door, followed by Margaret and Dave.

Once outside, both Margaret's and Dave's hearts skipped a beat. The land was lush, green, and gorgeous.

Danielle stood on the back step in her high heels. "If you two want to explore the property, I'll wait here and make some phone calls. I didn't come dressed to walk out there today," she said with a chuckle.

"Sounds good," Dave said as he grabbed Margaret's hand. He stopped and turned back to Danielle one last time. "You said the property back behind the trees is theirs too?"

Danielle nodded. "Yeah, it goes *way* back."

Margaret led the way, holding Dave's hand as they headed towards the tree line. After crossing to the other side, they were in a grassy meadow.

Dave pointed off to the right. "There's a huge pond back here. Think it's theirs?"

Margaret's eyes widened. "It has to be. We've only walked twenty-five feet from the tree line. Look! There's the blue heron standing in it."

They walked towards the pond and stared as two swans flew in and landed on the water.

Dave crossed his arms in awe. "Would you look at that? It's like your very own nature center out here."

Margaret squinted her eyes as she stared at something across the water. "What's that?"

Dave shielded his eyes from the sun to look. "Looks like stepping-stones."

Margaret squealed. "Let's see where they lead," she said as she pulled Dave to the other side.

They followed the stepping-stones through a shady area with more trees, and then back into a scene from a movie. There sat an old greenhouse made entirely of aged windows. The area around the greenhouse had overgrown blooming rose bushes in all colors and two crumbling birdbaths that still seemed to be of some use to the birds as one currently bathed in a couple inches of dirty water.

Margaret ran to the greenhouse and walked inside. Old flowerpots and potting soil were strewn about, and a few flower seeds must have dropped onto the ground because they bloomed through the rocks that lined the floor.

Dave took a deep breath as he walked inside the greenhouse with Margaret. "Wow. It's hot in here. It surely is a greenhouse."

Margaret's eye caught something on the other side of the yard. "Dave. Is that a … lighthouse?"

Dave stepped out of the greenhouse and stared in the direction Margaret looked. "Well, I'll be. It's a lighthouse replica. Looks to be about thirty feet tall."

Margaret giggled with happiness as she walked towards the lighthouse with Dave. They opened the small door and peered inside. It had a spiral staircase to the top, and many windows throughout. It even had stairs down to a basement area.

Margaret held a hand to her heart and looked Dave square in the eyes. "Dave, this is our home. This is it. I've never been surer in my life."

Dave nodded in agreement. "Oh, I know it is. We need to put an offer in today."

"Let's do it now," Margaret said, feeling impatient. "I don't want it to get away from us. I don't think we'll find something like this again for a long time."

Dave looked towards the farmhouse. "Let's go tell Danielle."

They walked back to the house where Danielle was still

standing on the step talking on her phone. She hung up just as they approached.

"Well, what do you think?" Danielle asked.

"We want to put in an offer," Dave said. "It's our dream home and property. By the way, we found a pond and greenhouse. Is that—"

Danielle smiled and cut in. "It is indeed part of the property. There's more beyond that too. You'll have to take a long look around next time. I knew this place would be perfect for you two. That's why I contacted you about it. Well, you guys can definitely put an offer in. Just know, though, I have more people coming to look at it today and tomorrow, and they may put offers in as well. I just want you both to be prepared for that."

Margaret felt her heart sink. What if someone gave the owners a better offer or even a cash offer? They couldn't compete with that.

Dave glanced at Margaret, then back at Danielle. "We're willing to try and do whatever it takes to get this place."

Danielle clapped her hands. "Perfect. I'll be in touch later today about putting together an offer letter for the seller, and we'll try and send it out before the day is over. In the meantime, here is the seller's email," she said as she handed a piece of paper to Margaret. "Maybe send a message to them after we submit the offer about why you want to buy the home and property," she said with a wink.

Margaret took the paper, folded it neatly, and put it in the pocket of her purse where she kept random seeds that she collected while out and about. This home was special to them, and now she needed to figure out how to explain that in an email to people she didn't know.

* * *

That evening, after everyone went to bed, Margaret sat at the kitchen table, and opened her laptop. Hours before, Danielle had emailed to let her know that their offer had been submitted and now it was a waiting game.

Margaret ran her fingers through her hair while staring at her computer screen. She had never wanted anything more in her life. Nothing felt more meant for her and Dave than this house. She needed to get it. She started typing.

Dear Mr. and Mrs. Lewis,

You don't know me, but my name is Margaret and my husband's name is Dave. I'm writing because we looked at your gorgeous farmhouse and property today and fell in love. We've been house hunting for over a month now, and nothing has felt more like a right fit for us and our family than your home.

You see, for two years now, we've been gardening on my sister's and brother-in-law's land here in Cape May. It's been incredible. Huge vegetables gardens, a sunflower field, and a little farm stand. It made us so happy, but we felt it was time to find our own farmland. A place we could marvel at as soon as we woke up. I envision us gazing out the kitchen window while we drink our coffee and having our hearts and souls feel so fulfilled.

I currently own my childhood home—the one my parents raised us in. It means the world to me, and giving that up in order to find something better was a very hard decision. I understand how leaving something that holds so many memories can be difficult, as I'm sure it was for you two and your family. The thing is my cousin from Arizona wants to purchase our home. Somehow, knowing that family is moving in and that they will respect and take care of the house has made it a whole lot easier.

I would just like to say that we are in love with your house and property and want to make it our forever home where we treat everything with love. We have put an offer in today with our realtor, and while we may not have the highest offer you will receive, I can assure you we have the best and most sincere intentions.

. . .

Sincerely,

Margaret Wilder Patterson

Margaret closed her laptop and took a long, deep sigh before standing up, pushing the kitchen chair back under the table, and taking one last look around the kitchen. She flicked off the light switch, and just as she was about to call it a night and walk upstairs to bed, an email notification went off on her phone.

"No. No, it can't be," Margaret said as she took out her phone and quickly clicked the email without looking.

Hydrangea Sale at Tom's Garden Center! 50% off!

Margaret's heart dropped. For a second, she'd thought it was a fast reply to her email to Mr. and Mrs. Lewis. Or maybe even an offer response from Danielle. She went to put her phone in her pajama pants pocket and looked at the email one last time.

"Hydrangeas, huh?" Margaret said with a smile. She paused a moment and envisioned their new home surrounded by purple, blue, and pink hydrangeas. It made her heart so happy.

Suddenly, she was overcome with dread. What if someone overbid them on the house? What if the owner's had a family friend that wanted the property? There was a chance they wouldn't get the house, and Margaret knew it. She could only hope that her email would help a little bit because they didn't have the extra money for a bidding war.

Dave sleepily walked down the stairs, rubbing his eyes, having just woken up. "I was wondering why you weren't in bed. What are you up to?"

Margaret sighed. "I wrote a letter to the owners. An email rather. I let them know how much we wanted the property. It's my last-ditch effort to get them to accept our offer. I think it was their daughter's email address. I hope she shows her parents. I'm so excited about the prospect of that house and property. I'm going to be so upset if we don't get it," Margaret said as she walked over to Dave and leaned her head on his chest.

Dave nodded. "What will be, will be. All we can do is try. Let's go get some rest," he said with a yawn.

CHAPTER FIVE

Days later, Sarah arrived nice and early at the dock to start her first shift on the birding boat.

As Chris hosed off the dock, he talked to a few other boat business owners who were cleaning off their boats next to him.

Sarah walked up behind him and nudged him, causing Chris to turn around.

"Good morning. Up early for the boat today, eh?" Chris said with a smile.

Sarah yawned and rubbed her eyes. "You could say that. When is everyone arriving?"

Chris looked at his watch. "Oh, not for an hour. We have to get the boat ready first. Do you mind taking that other hose over there and cleaning the floor of the boat?"

Sarah paused as she glanced at the hose that he pointed at. "Really?"

Chris chuckled. "Yeah, sure. It'll help me out a lot. I've still got to wipe down the binoculars and restock the boat's bathroom."

Sarah shrugged. "Alright. I can do that."

She turned on the hose and brought it onto the boat, pressing the nozzle's handle and practically power washing the floors with the force of the spray. Water, dirt, and debris flew everywhere, including all over her dry clothes.

Twenty minutes later, she walked over to Chris as he showed Natalie something with the register in the dock shop. Chris's eyes widened as Sarah stood before him dripping wet. "What happened?"

Sarah stared at Chris with annoyance. "You said to hose off the boat's floor. So I did that."

Chris tried to hide a chuckle. "Did you use the hard spraying mode on the nozzle or something?"

Sarah sighed, feeling gross in the wet shirt that clung to her skin. "Yes. How else will the dirt come off?"

Chris shook his head. "That wasn't necessary. The gentle setting would have worked just fine. It pushes the debris off into the drain."

Sarah stood there in silence, staring at Chris, not sure whether to scream or not.

Natalie interrupted. "I have a change of clothes. You're welcome to them."

Sarah kept staring at Chris. "No, that's not necessary. I'll run home really quick to change."

Just then, a few customers arrived, walking into the shop. Chris glanced at Natalie then at Sarah. "Maybe you should borrow her clothes. We're scheduled to leave here in ten minutes, and you'll miss the boat. I have to go quickly clean the binoculars and restock the bathroom. Time got away from me."

Sarah tried to force a smile as she glanced at Natalie. "I appreciate it, Natalie. I'll wash and return them tomorrow."

Natalie reached behind the register, pulled her backpack onto the counter, and took out a top and a pair of shorts, handing them over to Sarah. "Here you go. I think they'll fit you."

Sarah accepted the clothes with a smile, holding them far

away from her so they wouldn't get wet as she walked to the bathroom.

Five minutes later, she was next to Chris, who was busy talking to the people on his tour.

"We should see plenty of osprey. I know there're lots of nests that we'll pass on our ride," Chris said right as he glanced over to see Sarah talking to someone else.

Chris's eyes widened as he caught Sarah's eye.

"What?" Sarah asked.

Chris looked her up and down. "That's what Natalie gave you to wear?"

Sarah looked down at her crop top and cutoff booty shorts and laughed. "Yeah. It's this or wet clothing since I didn't have time to go home. I also had to let my hair down since I lost my hair tie somewhere around here."

Chris nodded, realizing that he'd never seen Sarah dress like that before.

"What? Is it too much?" Sarah asked, concern taking over her face. "I know it's not my style at all, but it is really comfortable. It fits nicely."

Chris smiled. "No, I think I like it. You look cute." A man on the boat nodded in agreement until his wife took notice and nudged him in the stomach. Chris started the boat up. "Sarah, do you mind untying the boat from the dock?"

Sarah smiled, hopped onto the dock, and untied the boat, then jumped back on board just in the nick of time as it floated away. Except she slipped and fell, and ended up sprawled out on the boat's deck.

"Are you OK?" Chris asked.

Sarah sat up, rubbing her leg. "That's going to be a nice bruise in a couple days."

Chris kneeled down next to her. "Did you seriously hurt yourself?"

Sarah shook her head. "I'm fine. Just a little shaken up and bruised," she said as she slowly stood up. "Maybe this job isn't a good one for me. I seem to be doing everything wrong."

Chris put his arm around her as he walked back and took the wheel again to steer the boat out onto the bay. "Nonsense. I think you're perfect for it. Give it some time."

* * *

Margaret and Dave took the day off from work and ended up at Longwood Gardens in Kennett Square, Pennsylvania. It was a drive, but worth it. It was one of Margaret's happy places, and she was in dire need of it.

It was a beautiful, sunny May afternoon, the girls were in school, and Margaret and Dave meandered through the indoor conservatory looking at all of the colorful flowers and lush plants.

Margaret bent over to smell a lily, then stood up and sighed. "I still haven't heard back from Danielle about the offer. I bet they got a ton of offers on that place."

Dave nodded as he started walking out of the room. "Well, it's been six days. We should give it some time."

Margaret followed Dave to an area with sweet-smelling rosebushes. It was sunny and humid, and it felt good on her skin. "Should we go back to looking at houses in case this falls through? I feel like everything's on hold on right now."

Dave bit his lip. "I guess we should. That's probably the smart thing to do."

They had been there about an hour and a half, and Margaret felt her stomach growl. "Did you want to leave and get something to eat?"

Dave smiled. "I thought you'd never ask. I'm assuming you want to go to Terrain?"

Margaret laughed. "How'd you know?"

Dave nudged her playfully. "Oh, I just know all of your happy places, I guess."

Twenty minutes later, they put their name in with the host and waited for a table while browsing next door at Terrain's garden center. It was one of the most gorgeous places to shop that Margaret had ever seen. There were plants, soaps, lotions, bread mixes, bowls, plates, books—you name it.

Margaret picked up a potted thyme plant, touched the leaves and sniffed her fingers. "This smells amazing. I think I need it. It's one of the few things I didn't winter sow."

Dave cocked his head. "What are you going to do with all those winter-sown jugs. The seeds have grown so much after you took the lids off."

Margaret sighed. "I should be planting them in the ground right now. I was hoping to hold off until we found a place, but who knows when that's going to happen. I'll probably give a bunch of them to Greg for his garden. I'm sure he'll appreciate it."

Dave nodded. "That sounds like a good plan."

Just then, a text came through on Margaret's phone. "Looks like our table is ready next door. I'm going to go pay for this potted thyme really quick."

After paying and walking next door to their seats in a greenhouse-looking area of the restaurant, they looked over the menus.

Margaret gazed above at the sunny glass roof and the hanging ferns and houseplants all around them. "I've always wanted a greenhouse. It's been a dream of mine."

Dave looked up at the ceiling. "I have to say, I loved the greenhouses we had on the farm while growing up. I do miss them."

"Hi there, I'm Molly and I'll be taking care of you today," their server began. "Can I start you two off with some drinks?"

Margaret smiled and glanced down at the menu. "I'll have the blood orange cinnamon spritzer."

"And I'll have an Arnold Palmer. Thank you," Dave said as he went back to looking at the menu.

"It looks like they're still serving brunch. I'm glad. I see a lot that I want," Margaret said scanning the menu.

Molly was back with the drinks in a flash, setting them down in front of them. "Were you about ready to order? Did you have any questions for me?"

Margaret nodded. "I think we're ready. I'm going to have the fried avocado Benedict."

Dave handed their menus to Molly. "And I'm going to have the free-range egg omelet."

"Perfect," Molly said as she hurried back to the kitchen.

Margaret sighed as she glanced around the restaurant again. "I'm so glad we came here. I needed this."

Just as Dave was about to speak, Margaret's phone chirped with a notification from her purse.

"Was that your phone?" Dave asked curiously.

Margaret waved her hand. "Probably. I'm pretty sure it's Liz texting me back. I asked her a question earlier today. I'll check it later."

Dave nodded. "Gotcha."

Fifteen minutes later, their scrumptious dishes arrived, and Margaret and Dave didn't waste a minute diving in. A few bites later, a notification alert sounded from Margaret's phone again.

Dave took a bite of his omelet as he watched Margaret ignore the sound. "Do you want to check that? Maybe it's important."

Margaret sighed and dropped her fork, then opened her bag on the floor and grabbed her phone. "I'm sure it's just Liz—"

Dave was silent as he watched Margaret's face, while she read the text to herself.

"This can't be happening," Margaret said. "Is this real?"

Dave finished chewing. "What? What's wrong?"

Margaret put the phone down and covered her face with her hands, then opened her fingers to peek through them at Dave. "We got the house."

Dave's eyes bugged out of his head. "What? Are you serious?"

Margaret removed her hands from her bright-red face, feeling full of happiness and adrenaline. "That text wasn't from Liz. It was Danielle. They accepted our offer."

In the crowed restaurant, they wanted to jump from their seats with joy, but there wasn't any room. Instead, Dave grabbed Margaret's hand across the table. "I can't believe it. Our dream is becoming a reality."

Margaret's eyes teared up. "Danielle said that they had many offers. There was even an offer well above ours, including from investors that I guess wanted to flip it. For some reason, they chose us. She seems beyond happy for us."

Dave smiled from ear to ear. "Did Danielle know that you did indeed send them an email? She was the one who gave you the idea."

Margaret shook her head. "I forgot to tell her, and she never asked. I'll have to mention it and thank her."

Dave gave Molly a motion for the check from across the room and took his last sip of his Arnold Palmer. "Well, I guess there's still a lot to do with inspections and the lender."

"And the deposit and final walk-through. Danielle said if everything goes smoothly, and we don't find any major repairs, we can probably close by late June. Let's cross our fingers," Margaret said as she watched Molly drop the check off at their table.

Dave nodded. "And probably call your cousin Audrey. Let them know our offer was accepted. This will help things move along with them buying your house."

Margaret nodded. "That's right. Oh, it's going to work out so nicely."

Dave paid, and they left the restaurant feeling even happier than they had when they arrived.

* * *

That evening, Judy and Bob finally made their way to Wesley's Drive-in Movie Theater in Bob's bright blue 1960 Chevrolet Impala convertible with the top down.

Bob pulled to the entrance of the theater where a high school kid greeted them and took their tickets. They drove to a parking spot right in front of the big screen among the other cars and dialed their radio to the correct station for the movie's audio.

Judy smiled as she watched Bob, full of excitement, look around the entire drive-in. It was full of families, couples, and friends out for the evening together. Some people sat in their cars, like Bob and Judy, and others set up folding chairs to sit in. Off to one side was a large snack stand where they served nachos, hot dogs, pizza, soft pretzels, ice cream, and of course, popcorn.

Bob glanced at Judy. "It's spectacular here. Did you want to check out the snack stand before the movie?"

"Sure," Judy said as she opened her car door and stepped out.

They headed to the concession stand and made their way to the front window. "I'll have two hot dogs please. With mustard," Bob said happily.

The person at the window pointed to the very long line behind them. "Sir, you'll have to get to the end of the line. These people are all waiting to order."

A couple standing in the line chuckled.

Bob was taken aback. "Oh, I'm so sorry. I didn't realize," he said as he took Judy's hand, and they walked all the way to the back of the line, becoming the twenty-fifth people to queue up.

Judy glanced at Bob. "This line isn't moving at all, and the movie is about to start. Why don't we forget this and go back to the car."

Bob sighed. "I'm really hungry though."

Judy glanced at the line. "How about we bring our own food next time. Pack a cooler."

The woman in front of them turned around. "You're not allowed to bring your own food here, unfortunately. They make most of their profit from the snack stand, I'm told."

Judy shook her head. "Well, if they're not going to allow you to bring food, they can at least try and get this line moving a little faster. Nobody wants to miss the movie to wait in line."

The woman shrugged. "It is, what it is, I guess. It's the only drive-in around."

Judy turned to Bob. "How about we eat dinner before we come next time. That'll solve that issue."

A light bulb went off in Bob's head. "I have an even better plan."

CHAPTER SIX

It was a beautiful, hot Memorial Day weekend. The kickoff of summer, it sure *felt* like it at eighty-three degrees and sunny.

Donna poured the oil into the funnel cake fryer, then wiped the sweat off her forehead with the back of her hand. She adjusted the small fan that blew on her, but it didn't make much of a difference. She studied the air-conditioning unit that worked overtime, and turned the temperature down to make it cooler, but it loudly sputtered before grinding to a halt.

"Great. The air conditioner just bit the dust," she said aloud as she tapped it in a last-ditch effort to get it back on.

Her phone rang, and she picked it up in a huff.

"Donna! How's it going on the boardwalk? Is the funnel cake stand all set?" Dale yelled over the loud bangs and sawing noises coming from the restaurant.

Donna looked out the food cart's window, noticing the crowds were really starting to pick up on the boardwalk. "It's a sauna in here, Dale. The air conditioner stopped working."

"You're kidding. I thought it had at least a few more years left in it. I bought it brand-new for Porridge back before we had central air put in a few years ago. I'll come by and bring a new one. I just need to tie up some loose ends here first."

Donna gave a sigh of relief. "Perfect. Once these fryers start going, it's going to get even hotter."

"Well, turn all of the fans on and open the back door to let a breeze through. I'll be there as soon as I can. I'll have to push it up the boardwalk with a dolly. See you soon," Dale said as he hung up.

Donna looked around the empty food cart. It was only her. They'd hired other employees over the past week, mostly college-aged students, but thinking they wouldn't open until Monday of the long weekend, they hadn't scheduled them for the other two days. Opening on the weekend had been Donna's idea. She wanted to work the stand on her own first to get a feel for everything without worrying about training.

A woman walked up to the window. "Can I have a strawberry shortcake funnel cake?"

Donna smiled. "I'm so sorry. We're not open yet. We should be in about thirty minutes if you want to come back."

The woman looked at her watch. "There's a funnel cake place that's open right next door. I'll just go there," she said annoyed as she walked away.

Donna sighed and started prepping the funnel cake fillings. She had chocolate sauce, Nutella, bananas, blueberries, strawberries, cheesecake, apples—you name it. There was anything you could possibly want on a funnel cake.

She did a few test batches of funnel cake in the hot fry oil, and they came out wonderfully. Crispy on the edges and soft and hot on the inside. She was starving, having not eaten breakfast, so she added some blueberries and whipped cream to the test batch and finished the entire thing in ten minutes.

Over thirty minutes later, the roller coasters on the pier across from her started running, *whooshing* by carrying screaming riders. The announcers at the game booths chatted up passersby, trying to entice them to throw softballs at milk jugs or rolls balls to get the horse to win the race. Then, it became a sea of people in bathing suits, shorts, and flip-flops.

Donna felt her stomach start to rumble as she watched a large family walk up to her stand and stare at the menu on the side.

The man held his wallet at the window. "Hi there. We're going to get six funnel cakes. Two Oreo, two strawberry, and two Nutella."

"Great. That will be fifty-four dollars," Donna said as she started getting to work on the funnel cakes. She poured the batter into the fry oil, and felt her stomach turn again. This time, even worse than last time. She quickly got all six of the funnel cakes made, then scrambled to find Tums in her purse. In doing so, she knocked half of the toppings she'd just prepped all over the floor of the food cart. Huffing silently, she searched for paper towels, which were nowhere to be found. At her wit's end, she stepped over the spillage and walked outside of the cart, taking a deep breath while tears formed in her eyes.

A voice came from the side of her. "You OK over there?"

Donna searched to see who'd said that.

"Over here! Hi! Donna? Is that you?" a woman said from the corn on the cob cart next to her.

Donna squinted her eyes to see. "Becky? Becky from Stockton? Oh my gosh, what are you doing here?"

Becky laughed as she stepped out of her food cart to greet Donna. "I picked up a little side job working my brother's corn cart this summer. Crazy, right? Are you working that funnel cake cart?"

Donna sighed deeply. "I am. It's my boyfriend's cart. I'm sort of taking it over for the summer. I'll tell you though, I already don't think it's going to work. It's hot in there. Like, really hot, and the air conditioner just broke—"

Becky cut in. "You have an air conditioner? You're lucky. There isn't any room for one in my tiny cart. I'm getting by with the ocean breeze. So far so good."

Donna shook her head. "I wish I could get a breeze in

there. I've tried everything. Opening doors, positioning the fans differently ..."

Becky smiled. "I'm sure you'll figure it out."

Just then, a gaggle of high schoolers stood in front of the funnel cake cart, and all of the toppings were still spilled all over the floor.

"Oh geez. I've gotta tell these people that the cart is down. I just spilled all my toppings," Donna said as she walked inside the cart.

Becky, noticing customers coming towards the corn cart, also headed back.

"I'm sorry, but we're having a little malfunction. You may want to go next door for funnel cakes," Donna said to the high schoolers. They all shrugged and walked away.

Donna reached up into the cabinet, finally remembering where the paper towels and spray were stored, and started cleaning up the mess all over the floor.

"Knock, knock," Dale said as he tapped on the cart.

Donna peered towards the door. "Oh my gosh, Dale. I'm so glad to see you."

Dale looked at the mess on the floor Donna was cleaning up and chuckled. "I guess the first day is not going as planned, huh."

Donna stood up and threw the dirty paper towels into the trash can behind the cart. "You could say that."

Dale hoisted the air conditioner into the cart and started removing the old one with the tools in his back pocket.

"Can you hand me that wrench I just left on the counter there," Dale asked.

Donna handed him the wrench, then stared in silence, watching Dale take the old AC unit out and put the new one in.

"That about does it," Dale said as he turned the new unit on, feeling the cold air bursting out of it. "Works like a dream too."

Donna sighed as she bent down to get the old AC unit off the floor and walked it outside to the dolly.

"Hey, I could have done that. It's really heavy," Dale said, impressed by Donna's strength.

Donna shrugged. "It's fine. I can get it."

Dale grabbed Donna's hand. "Are you OK? You seem a little down."

Donna looked off into the distance towards the ocean. "I don't think this is for me. I'm not enjoying it at all."

Dale rubbed her back. "Look, my advice is to give it more time. I think opening day is always a little hectic, and it's a bad time to assess your feelings. I remember how crazy it was when I opened. Give it some time, then if you don't like it, that's fine. Don't feel obligated to do it for me."

A couple hours later, Greg opened his trunk and pulled out a crate of fresh-picked lettuce, peas, kale, and radishes from the garden. He closed the trunk then stood on the street and looked at Heirloom, his pride and joy. The front porch was beautifully set with tables, chairs, hanging ferns, and white drapes pulled tight at each corner. The trees that lined the street created lots of shade that kept everything feeling cooler, though it was hot.

He glanced down at the corner, noticing a dumpster on the street and many construction trucks.

Jack, his cook, met him on the street and took the crate of vegetables from him. "Wow. This is everything from the garden?"

Greg nodded. "Yep. You guys all helped grow this. I'm pretty sure you were the one who planted the radish and lettuce seeds."

Jack smiled. "That's so cool. I really enjoyed being out

there planting things. Never did it before. I was always a city boy until I moved out here."

Greg patted him on the back. "Come out any time. Maybe we can make a schedule with the rest of the staff for what days everyone wants to come help on the farm."

"I think they'd like that," Jack said as he walked inside with the crate.

Greg took a deep breath of the cool breeze that suddenly blew in and stood quietly as he listened to the birds sing. That was all cut short when a table saw, presumably down at the corner restaurant, started making ear-piercing noise.

Greg shook his head in annoyance. Such ruckus didn't make for a peaceful dining atmosphere. Hopefully, they'll be done before 5 p.m. when the restaurant opens, Greg thought to himself.

Jack suddenly appeared on the porch again, this time empty-handed. "Greg, did you go want to go over the specials before we start prepping?"

Greg nodded as he kept his eyes on the corner restaurant. "That sounds good. I'll be inside in a second. Say, Jack …"

"Yeah?" Jack asked, as he glanced down the block to where Greg was looking.

"Do you know what's going on at the corner restaurant there? Did Grandmother's Gravy close?" Greg asked.

Jack nodded. "That's what I heard. I guess someone else bought the space. I'm not sure what's going in there," he said as he headed back inside after somebody called for him.

Greg sighed as he watched a construction crew walk out of the restaurant space, retrieve tools from their truck, and then walk back inside.

The quiet lull in the air was once again interrupted by not only a table saw, but also nonstop hammering. Greg glanced one more time towards the corner before walking inside Heirloom. This time, out of the corner of his eye, he noticed a familiar form.

"Dale?" Greg said aloud to nobody. He stared, wanting to get a better look, but it was too late. The guy was already out of sight.

Greg furrowed his brow as he pulled the door open and headed back to the kitchen.

Ron, one of the chefs, was busy washing and cutting the lettuce. "Heard you saw the construction going on over at Grandmother's Gravy."

Greg nodded as he walked to the coffee machine full of freshly brewed coffee and poured himself a cup. He took a sip. "You could say that. Do you happen to know what's going in there?"

Ron started shelling the peas and handed the lettuce over to Jack to dry. "It's another restaurant. That's all I've heard; I don't know much else. I tried asking the construction crew when I walked by, but they didn't have any details other than that."

"Huh," Greg said. "It's weird because I swear I just saw my friend Dale walk inside of that place. But if it's his restaurant, why wouldn't he have told me? He knows Heirloom is only three doors down."

Ron stopped shelling peas. "Did Dale tell you he was looking to open a restaurant in Cape May?"

"Yes, he did," Greg said matter-of-factly.

Ron shrugged. "Well, there's your answer."

Greg shook his head. "I don't get it though."

Jack walked out of the kitchen and sat at a nearby dinner table. "Are we ready to go over specials now?"

"That's right. We should probably do that now before we forget," Greg said, as he quickly snapped out of his thoughts.

* * *

Margaret was at home, finishing up fundraising work for the wildlife refuge for the day, when she received a phone call.

"Hey, Mom," Margaret said as she closed her laptop and walked into the kitchen.

"Hi, there. Have you heard from Audrey and Rob today?" Judy asked as she folded the freshly dried towels.

"No, why?" Margaret asked.

"Well, I just got off the phone with Audrey. She told me that Rob's job is now starting June 15 instead of the thirtieth. So, now they have to get to Cape May earlier."

Margaret scratched her head. "We don't close on our house until the twenty-second, and that's move-in day."

Judy nodded. "Right. I told her that. They were scrambling to come up with temporary housing, but they'll have all their stuff with them. They're driving across country in a moving truck. It's a tricky situation."

Margaret thought for a moment. "I don't know what to do. Putting our stuff in storage for a week is going to be a lot of extra work and money. We have movers coming on the twenty-second already. By the fifteenth we'll be in full packing mode, and the house will be a mess."

Judy finished folding the last towel and put it on top of the others in the closet. "Well, I think I'll tell them to come stay here with us. We have the guest bedroom. They can leave everything in the moving truck and just bring inside their clothes and toiletries. We'll have to set up an air mattress for Bonnie."

"You think that will work?" Margaret asked.

"I hope so," Judy said. "Greg's extended family will be staying at their house that week, so that's not an option. You said Dave's beach house is rented out, and your house will be in disarray from packing. I think it's the best option."

Margaret gave a sigh of relief. "OK. Well, let me know when you talk to them about it. Hopefully, that works for them."

Judy nodded as she walked into the kitchen to check on the crockpot chicken meal that had been cooking all day. "I think it will work out fine. By the way, have you told Abby and Harper about moving yet? I know you were waiting to pop the news."

Margaret shook her head. "We haven't. We were waiting until everything was official, and now it is. I guess it's probably time. I'm a little scared of how upset they'll be. They've lived in this house their entire lives."

"It'll be fine. It will all be fine. I'm going to call Audrey now. We'll talk later," Judy said as she hung up.

Margaret put her phone back into her pocket as Abby and Harper appeared in the kitchen.

"Was that Grandma? What did she say?" Harper asked curiously.

Margaret nodded. "Oh, she was just saying hi. How do you two feel about pizza for dinner?"

Abby and Harper jumped for joy as Margaret suddenly felt guilty about keeping the girls out of the loop with the move.

CHAPTER SEVEN

Margaret opened the kitchen cabinet and pulled out several appliances. A blender, food processor, juicer, and iced-tea maker. She wiped them off before placing them into a moving box.

Meanwhile, Dave was in the living room, taking books off the shelf. He opened one and stared at it. "Are we packing *everything* for this move?" Dave asked as he looked up at the hundreds of books on the shelf that hadn't been touched since they were first read.

Margaret sighed as she got up off the kitchen floor and walked to Dave, also staring at the books. "I'm never going to read these again. I don't know why I save them. Pack them all up and we can donate them."

Dave shrugged. "Whatever you want."

Margaret looked around the house, realizing how much more they had to pack in only a few weeks' time. She made her way back to the kitchen box she had just filled.

Dave taped up the box full of books and headed for the back door. He stopped and turned to look at Margaret who was still adding kitchen items to her box.

"Can we please tell the girls about the move now? It's June

4, and escrow closes June 22. We're running out of room for more storage in the garage, and we need to start using the house," Dave said.

Margaret sighed as she taped her box shut. "You're right. This has dragged on too long. Hiding all this from the girls in the garage can't go on forever. We'll tell them after school tonight, but I'm not looking forward to it. The girls grew up in this house. Heck, so did I. There're so many memories here."

Dave nodded. "I get it. I really do. It was rough when my parents sold the farm we grew up on, but it did work out in the end. Now my brother and sister-in-law live there, and we even got to grow a garden on the property."

Margaret smiled. "And now Audrey, Rob, and Bonnie are coming to live here. I'm sure we'll be visiting often. I'll explain all of this to the girls. Hopefully, it'll help ease their broken hearts."

Sarah boarded the Blue Heron birding boat with a backpack strapped to her shoulders and two coffees and a bag with bagel breakfast sandwiches in her hands.

Chris stopped cleaning the windows to look at over at Sarah. "Hey! You got here early."

Sarah smiled as she handed him a coffee and a bacon, egg, and cheese sandwich. "I did. I'm so excited. It's going to be a gorgeous day."

Chris chuckled. "It is indeed."

Sarah stowed her backpack in the back corner of the boat and walked over to Chris. "Give me something to do. I'm ready to get to work."

Chris thought for a moment. "Why don't you wipe down the binoculars."

"Easy enough," Sarah said as she found the wipes and got to work.

Ten minutes later, people began boarding the boat for their morning cruise on the water. Sarah enthusiastically greeted everyone. "Good morning. Are you all ready to be out on the serene water, seeing all the gorgeous shorebirds?"

Chris smiled at Sarah, his heart warmed at seeing his girlfriend work so well with the customers. He took the wheel and started the boat up.

"I'll untie the boat from the dock," Sarah said as she made her way to the front of the boat.

Moments later, Chris was giving his spiel to the customers as he backed the boat out of the dock and cruised out towards the bay.

"What's that bird?" a woman asked.

Chris looked out the window as he steered. "That's a white egret."

Another woman pointed next to Sarah. "And what's that?"

Sarah fumbled on her words. "Oh … I've never seen that one before. That's …"

Chris glanced over their shoulders. "That's a cormorant."

Suddenly a couple large boats went by, their wakes caused the Blue Heron to sway and bob.

"Hold tight, everyone. It's going to get a little rocky for a minute," Chris said.

The boat rocked back and forth, and Sarah felt her breakfast sandwich turn in her stomach. She ran to the bathroom, slammed the door shut, and did not come out for ten minutes. When she finally emerged, she found a cushion towards the back of the boat and sat with her hood pulled up over her head and her sunglasses on.

Chris pointed to some blue herons flying over them before noticing Sarah at the back of the boat. He walked over to her. "You OK?"

Sarah shook her head. "Not really. I probably shouldn't have eaten something right before I got on the boat."

Chris rubbed her back. "I've got some ginger ale. That might help. Want some?"

Sarah nodded. "I guess I could sip on it."

Chris came back with the ginger ale, handing it to Sarah before touching her back again. "Let me know if you need anything else. We have an hour left of the tour. I'll try and stay on calm water, though I can't help when a boat passes."

"I know. Thank you for that. Though, I'm starting to think helping out on the boat isn't for me. Between getting soaked hosing down the deck, falling on the deck, and now getting seasick," Sarah said as she took a sip of the soda.

Chris nodded, feeling a little bummed. "I get it. Do what's best for you, but I do love having you out here," he said as he walked back to the steering wheel.

Sarah took a long, deep breath as she looked out the window. Out of the corner of her eye, she noticed something yellow on the bench next to her. It was a New Jersey birding book. She picked it up and started reading as the bay breeze blew in through the window.

An hour later, Chris pulled the boat back into the dock while Sarah was still reading. The customers all got off the boat, and Chris walked back to Sarah.

"We're back. You can finally get off the boat," he said with a chuckle.

Sarah closed the book. "Is it OK if I take this book home? I've been learning a ton. I identified every bird I saw while we were out on the water using this book. It's fantastic."

Chris smiled ear to ear. "You most definitely can. That book is pretty special to me. I found it in an old bookshop many years ago. Did you notice all the penciled-in notes everywhere? It was a well-loved book before it was donated, and it's how I first learned about all the shorebirds out here."

Sarah grabbed Chris's hand in hers as she popped out of her seat. "I did notice. I knew it wasn't your handwriting. I love that you learned from this book. Now let's get off this boat before I feel sick again," Sarah said with a chuckle.

* * *

Greg was off from work and getting dirty in the garden with some of the other kitchen staff. His phone rang as he staked some cherry tomatoes.

"Hey, Dale. What's going on?" Greg asked as he stood up and bent backward to stretch out his back.

"Oh, you know. Just trying to get this new restaurant up and running. How's Heirloom doing?" Dale asked as he got out of his car and walked into Monarch Coffeehouse.

"Oh, it's going. Business is great. We're out in the garden—my chef, cooks, and I, and even some servers are helping out. Everyone seems to love it out here. Why don't you come on out here one day? Pick some produce, and maybe get a little dirty."

Dale looked at his watch. "Oh, I don't know … everything is so busy lately."

Greg scratched his head. "You haven't said much about the restaurant. Did you find a space?"

Dale paused. "I did. It's a great place to have a restaurant too. They've started construction on it."

"Oh yeah? Whereabouts?" Greg asked.

Dale, stammered, still unsure about how Greg would feel about his restaurant being so close to his. "Well, um … it's in Cape May. Great location."

Greg chuckled. "Yes, I know that, but *where* in Cape May?"

Dale scratched his head in thought as he stepped into the line to order. "It's over on the other side of the main hub. You know, outside of the downtown area."

Greg paused, starting to sense that Dale was avoiding the question. "That's really vague, Dale. Can you be more specific?"

Dale felt his heart drop as he stood in line for coffee. The customer in front of him paid, and it was his turn. Suddenly, relief fell over him. "Hold on, Greg. I'm about to put in my coffee order. I stopped over at Monarch."

Greg heard Dale talking to the barista for a few moments.

When Dale got back on the phone, he said, "Hey. Can I call you back? I'm juggling a tray of coffee here for the construction crew."

Greg nodded. "No problem, but I want to hear all about this restaurant."

Dale gave a nervous laugh. "You got it."

Greg hung up the phone just as Liz walked outside with a tray of homemade lemonade.

"I brought you all some cold drinks," Liz said as she handed out the glasses.

Greg took a long sip and sighed as the sun beat down on him. "Thank you, Liz. This hit the spot. Why don't you come join us for a little bit. I'm telling you, being out here feels great."

Liz shook her head. "I don't think so, Greg. I don't know if it's my thing."

Greg cocked his head. "You were so excited about planting flowers out here. What happened with that? And when Dave and Margaret had the garden, you loved helping out with the farm stand."

Liz shrugged. "Ruining my expensive shoes in mud and getting completely dirty and attacked by bugs happened."

Greg chuckled and put his hand on her shoulder. "Come on. Give it another shot. Wear gardening shoes and clothes you don't mind getting dirty. Apply a little bug spray."

Liz sighed as she looked back at the house. "Fine. I'll go in and change, but I'm not going to be out here all day. I still have work to get done."

Greg smiled from ear to ear. "I can't wait," he said as he bent down to tie another tomato plant to the stake he'd already put in the ground.

Ten minutes later, Liz was back, reeking of bug spray and wearing clogs, a shirt with paint all over it, and a baseball cap. "Here I am. Give me something to do."

Greg reached into his pocket and pulled out a large packet of mixed flower seeds. "The guys just cleared out that plot over there for flowers. Just broadcast these over the soil, then gently rake them in."

Liz took the seeds from Greg and looked them over. "Sounds a little boring, but I can do that, I guess."

Greg thought for a moment as Liz walked toward the flower garden plot. "Hey, Liz?"

"Yeah?" Liz asked as she turned around fifteen feet away.

"Do you know anything about Dale's new restaurant? Where it is? Did Donna say anything to you?"

Liz shook her head. "Nope. Haven't heard much about it, and I forgot to ask."

Greg scratched his head. "Huh, OK."

Liz stared at Greg, who looked confused. "Why do you ask?"

Greg bent down to pull a weed. "He's avoiding telling me for some reason. I asked him today outright, and he was super vague. It's so odd. I don't know why he's being like that."

Liz shrugged. "Weird. I'm sure there's a good reason. Maybe he wants to surprise everyone?"

Greg chuckled. "Maybe, but I don't know about that."

* * *

After dinner, Margaret, Dave, Harper, and Abby went to Peace Pie for ice cream sandwiches. They weren't your traditional ice cream sandwiches, as they also had a layer of pie filling in them, which they all loved.

Everyone ordered, and found a bench to sit on, while Dave stood behind them, eating his salted caramel apple pie ice cream sandwich. He glanced at Margaret, signaling to her that maybe now was a good time to discuss the move with the girls.

Margaret nodded at Dave, then cleared her throat. "Girls, while you eat your ice cream sandwiches, we have something to talk to you about. It's a bit of a big thing."

Abby took a bite of her chocolate mint. "OK."

Harper nodded but didn't say anything.

"Well, you know how Dave and I have a garden at Aunt Liz and Uncle Greg's?"

"Yeah?" Harper said as she bit into her cookie dough sandwich.

"Well, after Dave and I got married last year, we dreamed of having our own farmland and property to start fresh on," Margaret said as she glanced up at Dave with a smile.

Abby put her Peace Pie down. "Are we moving?"

Harper rolled her eyes. "Yes, we're moving. Remember when we were playing outside and saw all those boxes in the garage?"

Abby shrugged. "I don't know."

Harper turned to look at Margaret and Dave. "I figured we were moving. I just didn't know when. I'm fine with it."

Margaret widened her eyes. "What? You are? Are you just saying that, Harp? I want to know the truth."

Harper took another bite. "I thought about it, and I'm ready for a new bedroom. My own bedroom. I think I'm too old to share a bedroom with my sister."

Abby crinkled her nose. "Hey! That's not nice."

Dave laughed. "Well, you two chose to share a room, remember? There is an extra bedroom that you could have moved into."

Harper sighed. "Well, now you tell me."

Abby started to cry. "I don't want to move. I love our house."

Dave squeezed next to Abby and put his arms around her

for a hug. "Mom still has to tell you the good news about the house though."

Margaret nodded as she touched Abby's hand. "Your cousin Bonnie and Aunt Audrey and Uncle Rob are moving into our house. They're coming all the way from Arizona to move here. We'll still be able to visit, and you can play in the yard. You will still get to be there."

Abby wiped her tears away. "Bonnie is moving here?"

Margaret's eyes got watery. "Yes. Isn't that great? Family is moving into our home."

Harper stood up and casually stretched. "Well, when are we moving? I have a schedule to keep."

Margaret and Dave laughed.

"June 22 is when we'll get the keys to the house, so that's when we can move in. We've got a lot of packing to do," Margaret said.

Dave chuckled. "And now we can stop sneaking around. It's time to go full force. We'll need help from both of you. Are you ready?"

Abby jumped up next to Harper. "Yes!"

Margaret glanced at Dave, her heart feeling happy and relieved all at once.

CHAPTER EIGHT

It was June 11 and Audrey, Rob, and Bonnie arrived in Cape May with their large moving truck rental that they'd driven across country and now were bringing their suitcases into Bob and Judy's little two-bedroom rancher.

"Oh my goodness! You're here!" Judy yelled out as she opened the front door and gave Audrey, Rob, and Bonnie hugs.

Bob walked out from the kitchen with Hugo at his heels. "Hello, everyone! How was the drive?"

Audrey chuckled. "Let's just say we're glad to finally be here."

Rob nodded in agreement. "I think we drove through at least three terrible storms during that drive. At one point, we were on a bridge, and I could feel the truck swaying in the wind. I was holding on for dear life."

Judy grabbed Audrey's suitcase from her hands. "Well, you're here and safe, and that's all that matters now. Follow me this way, I'll show you to your room."

Judy opened the door to the small homey bedroom with a queen-size bed and a dresser. "Here you are. I also have an air mattress to put at the foot of the bed for Bonnie."

Bonnie peeked her head through the adults to see. "I guess it will work, but what about Doug? Where will he sleep?"

Bob scratched his chin out in the hallway. "Doug? Is there another child I don't know about?"

Rob laughed. "No, Bonnie's our only human child, but we do have a fur-child now. And Doug is still sitting in the front seat of the truck. I left it running with the AC on. Audrey, I thought you told them about Doug," he said as he glanced over at his wife.

Audrey nervously laughed. "I … thought I did?"

Judy cleared her throat. "Well … the more the merrier. Our old dog, Hugo, might enjoy the company. How old is Doug?"

Bonnie cut in. "A puppy! Let's go get him," she said as she ran to the front door.

Rob shrugged as he turned to the adults. "I'll be right back. Going to get the dog."

Moments later, the most rambunctious miniature golden-doodle puppy panted with excitement and tried to run full force into the house despite being on a leash.

Hugo stood behind Bob's legs as Doug eyed him up like a fresh tennis ball from across the room. Rob held a dog crate in the other arm. "You won't have to worry about Doug. For now, since he's a puppy, he's being crate trained. He'll go in here at night to sleep or if we all leave the house. It keeps him safe, and he likes it. As he gets older and more trusted alone, we'll stop using it."

Bob nodded. "Whatever works," he said as he walked to the bathroom and closed the door.

Bonnie looked up at Audrey. "Mom, I have to pee."

Audrey smiled. "OK, honey." She glanced at Judy. "Is there another bathroom in the house?"

Judy shook her head. "No, just the one. Hopefully, we can all figure out a schedule that works. Sharing one bathroom between five people might get tricky."

Rob nodded. "We'll work it out. We're only here eleven days."

Bonnie stared up at Rob. "I have to go, Dad. Like, *really* go."

Judy impatiently glanced at the bathroom door. "He should be out in a minute."

Five minutes later, Bob emerged from the bathroom with everyone staring at him. "What?" he asked, surprised. "I was shaving."

Judy smacked her forehead. "Dear. Could you have waited to do that until after our traveling guests could use the bathroom?"

Bob shrugged as Bonnie rushed past him into the bathroom and closed the door. "I didn't even think of it. I'm so sorry."

Audrey chuckled as she picked up Doug who was still the most excited jumpy puppy in the world. "It's OK. She only went ten million times during the drive. I think that child drinks too much."

Hugo came back into the room with the adults from the kitchen after eating some kibble from his food bowl. Just then, Doug jumped out of Audrey's arms and charged towards Hugo. Hugo darted across the room and stood behind the couch, unsuccessfully trying to hide.

Bob and Judy laughed. "It's OK, Hugo. He won't hurt you. He's just a puppy."

Hugo, who was up there in age, wasn't thrilled about the new visitor. He would stare at Doug as he jumped on him trying to play and then stare back at Judy and Bob as if to say, "Really? You're doing this to me?"

Rob scooped Doug up. "Alright little guy, you're going outside to pee, and then for a walk to expend this pent-up energy," he said with a chuckle.

Judy looked out the front door towards the truck. "So, everything is packed in that truck?"

Audrey stepped next to her and looked outside. "Yep. Our whole house. We have a padlock on the back, but it will stay there until move-in day."

Judy smiled as she put her hand on Audrey's shoulder. "I hope you're all hungry. I have sandwiches, chips, fruit, and sides."

Audrey gave a sigh of relief. "I'm starving. Thank you, Judy. We appreciate the hospitality."

* * *

After a little learning curve, Donna finally had the funnel cake stand running like a well-oiled machine. Her staff had been trained, and for the most part, everything was working out.

As her two employees made the funnel cake batter and restocked the cart, Donna stared off towards the ocean in a daze. A breeze blew in, carrying the salty ocean smell with it, and suddenly working the funnel cake stand seemed like a dream come true. She was being paid to practically hang out on the beach, even if it was twenty-five feet away.

She smiled and felt something funny on her toe, and she looked down to see that one of her brand-new expensive flip-flops had broken. The one on her right foot, to be exact.

"Oh, no," Donna said as she kneeled down, trying to fix the flip-flop to no avail.

"That stinks," Olivia, one of her new employees, said as she glanced down.

Josh, her other employee, nodded in agreement.

"You're telling me," Donna said as she took off the flip-flop and chucked it into the trash.

Suddenly, a loud noise came from the new air conditioner, and it sputtered off. Except it wasn't the only thing to turn off—all of the electric in the cart went out at once.

"Great," Donna said, frustrated. "Guys, wait here. I'm going to go and find someone that can help get the power back on. Tell any customers that we can't serve anything right now."

Olivia nodded. "Sure thing."

Donna took off on foot, with only the one flip-flop, and walked down the sunny boardwalk, trying to figure out where to find someone who could help. It was extra hot and the sun beat down on her as she wiped sweat off her forehead.

"Ow!" she screamed and looked down at her bare foot. It now had a huge wood splinter in it from the boardwalk.

She took of the other flip-flop off, threw it in the trash, then found a bench, and quickly sat down, trying—unsuccessfully—to remove the splinter.

Ten minutes later, she was up and hobbling barefoot back to the funnel cake cart, looking red as a lobster.

"Um … how did it go?" Josh asked when he noticed Donna looking very frustrated as she stood by the window of the cart.

"It didn't. I'm going to send you two home for the day because I don't know when we're going to get electric back. Is that OK?" Donna asked.

Olivia grabbed her bag out of the cabinet. "Well then, I'm going straight to the beach."

Josh laughed. "Say no more. I'm happy to have the day off as well," he said as he hopped out of the cart next to Donna.

"Thank you, guys. I'll see you again next weekend," Donna said, her foot throbbing and her skin stinging.

Suddenly, a voice could be heard behind her. "Donna!"

Donna turned around to see Becky back on the corn cart. "Hey, Becky, how's it going?" Donna asked, trying to force a smile.

Becky shrugged as she handed an *elote* corn on the cob to a customer. "It's going. Just got here. How's the funnel cake business going?"

Donna laughed and shook her head. "Awful. I just sent my employees home because our electric is out."

Becky frowned. "That stinks. Why don't you come pull up a stool, have some corn, and talk to me to let some steam off."

Donna smiled genuinely. "That sounds great," she said as she hobbled over onto a stool in the shade under the umbrella.

"Hello, miss. What can I getcha? It's on the house," Becky said jokingly.

Donna stared up at the menu on the whiteboard above her. "Hmm ... the lime basil butter corn sounds great."

"Coming right up!" Becky yelled as she quickly pulled out a hot corn on the cob, brushed butter all over it, then squeezed lime and sprinkled it with fresh basil, before handing the whole thing to Donna with napkins.

Donna nodded as she took a bite. "Oh my gosh. This is divine. This is just what I needed, Becky. Thank you."

Becky rubbed her hands together. "Sure thing. So, are you only doing the funnel cake on the weekends?"

"Yep. They're the best business days until school gets out next week. Then, I'll probably do some weekdays too. What about you?" Donna asked as she took another bite.

Becky tightened her ponytail then leaned on the counter outside the ordering window. "Same. Though I have done a few weekdays here and there. Oh, look, there's Brett. Brett!"

Donna turned around to see a young guy walking over with about fifty keys dangling from a key ring clipped to his belt loop.

"Hello, ladies. How's it going, Becky? Everything OK since we moved your cart off that bump in the wood?" Brett asked.

Becky sighed. "Oh, you don't even know. Ten times better. Everything is level in the cart now. I don't have to worry about the corn sliding off the counter," she said with a chuckle.

Donna glanced at Becky then at Brett.

"Oh my gosh! How could I forget? Brett, this is Donna. She works the funnel cake stand, and her electric just went out. Is there any way you could help with that?" Becky asked.

Brett rolled his eyes. "For real? This happened on

Wednesday with the french fry cart over there. I think I know the culprit. Let me go check," Brett said as he walked off.

Becky nodded at Donna. "He'll take care of it. He's a good guy. Not sure what his title is, but he works the boardwalk."

Five minutes later, Brett was back and shaking his head. "Well, it was what I thought it was. Your electric is back on, Donna, and I made sure it won't happen again."

"Thank you so much, Brett. I'm relieved, but what was it?"

Brett sighed deeply. "The new fruit cart behind you plugged into your dedicated outlet and overloaded it. I showed them where their outlet for power is, but they must have someone new working today. I labeled your outlet, so it shouldn't happen again. Alright, I'm off. Have a good one," Brett said as he took off, his hefty key ring jangling loudly against his leg.

Becky clapped her hands. "There you have it."

Donna laughed. "I guess I shouldn't have sent my staff home, but I can handle the cart alone. May have to close a little early, though," Donna said as she stood up from the stool.

"Hey!" Becky yelled after her.

"Yeah?" Donna said as she turned around.

"Let's get cheeseburgers after work, then walk it off on the boards. What do you say?" Becky asked with excitement behind her voice.

Donna shrugged and chuckled. "Sure. I'll probably be too tired to cook anyway, and Dale will be working late."

* * *

That evening, Greg loosened his tie and took a deep breath as he walked outside once Heirloom had closed after a busy night. He was the last one out, and the warm evening full of crickets chirping felt like bliss on his tired body.

He clicked his fob to unlock his car but nothing happened. He clicked it again. Nothing.

"What in the world?" Greg said out loud, confused when his car wasn't parked close by.

Suddenly, he remembered he'd parked around the block due to lack of spaces. As he slowly trudged down the sidewalk, he noticed that the restaurant on the corner was lit up like a Christmas tree.

Greg got closer and his eyes widened as he saw all the work that had been done to the place. It looked absolutely incredible. A tiny part of him was almost jealous even. Why hadn't he thought of this design?

The front part of the restaurant had a roll-up garage-style door that could be lifted up in the summer or fall to make it an open-air restaurant. Inside was a what looked like a partially stocked farm market full of jars of locally made jam, tomato sauce, pickles, and other such things. Around the farm market was also a restaurant with rustic wood farm tables and chairs. Towards the back stood an open-concept kitchen with a counter and stools for patrons to eat while watching food being cooked in front of them. Then, there was the wooden bar in the other far corner.

As Greg walked inside, looking to talk to someone, Dale walked out from the back, talking to one of the construction crewmen.

"OK, so, 8 a.m. tomorrow? See the crew then?" Dale said as he shook Joe's hand.

"You got it. We should have this place finished within the week. Gosh, it looks great," Joe said as he took one last look around, then left.

Dale stood with his back to Greg, having no idea he was there.

"Hey," Greg said.

Dale whipped around. "Whoa, you made my heart jump," he said as he caught his breath.

"Is this your place? The one you were being vague about?"

Dale looked down at his feet. "You could say that."

Greg crossed his arms as he walked around the place, eyeballing everything top to bottom. "Why didn't you tell me you were three doors down from Heirloom?"

Dale shrugged and pulled out a chair to sit in. "I don't know .... Well, honestly, I thought you were going to be mad at how close I was to you. I didn't want you think I was trying to take away your customers."

Greg laughed as he pulled up a seat next to Dale and sat down. "Take away my customers? Get out of here with that nonsense! Do you see all the restaurants near other restaurants in Cape May that do perfectly fine? If anything, I think it will drive more traffic to Heirloom. I think it will be *good* for business—for both of us."

Dale's face lit up. "You really think that?"

Greg nodded. "I do, but I have a great idea for the market area of the restaurant. Come help out in the garden and you can sell the produce here. Fresh tomatoes, basil, peppers, and squash. Just think about it, will ya?"

Dale jumped out of his seat, full of excitement. "You know, I've been pondering that idea. I think I'm sold. When can I start in the garden?"

Greg thought for a moment. "Come by next week. The whole gang will be there. It'll be a blast."

Dale paused as he looked at the wall covered in framed dog portraits, vinyl records, and sheet music. "I can't wait to show Donna this."

Greg chuckled. "She hasn't seen it?"

Dale shook his head. "Not yet. I told her I wanted her to wait for the grand reveal. She's been hustling at the funnel cake stand, and I'm proud of her. I have something special for us planned."

CHAPTER NINE

It was finally the day before Margaret and Dave's house closed escrow, and thus moving day eve for both Margaret and Dave and Rob and Audrey.

Judy sat in her chair on the front porch and called Margaret. "Hi there, what are you all up to?" she asked as she took a sip of her peach iced tea.

Margaret laughed as she looked at the stacks of boxes taking over the kitchen. "We're packing away over here. Just about finished, thankfully."

"Oh, that's great. Rob, Audrey, and Bonnie seem eager to move in," Judy said.

Margaret nodded. "We spoke yesterday. They're as excited as we are. Hopefully, everything goes smoothly."

Judy changed the subject. "Anyway, the reason I'm calling is to see if you wanted to take a break this evening and go to bag bingo with me?"

Margaret felt exhaustion set in. "I don't know about that, Mom. We still have a bunch more to do before tomorrow."

Judy cut in. "Audrey's coming, and so is Liz. I also have two extra tickets if you want to invite Sarah and Donna. Just think

—bingo, basket auctions, fifty-fifty raffle, wine and snacks … and the girls."

Margaret stopped and thought for a moment, then looked at Dave as he came in from the yard. "Dave, do you think I'll be able to go to bingo for a few hours without slowing us down?"

Dave nodded. "Definitely. We're way ahead because we stayed up packing all night. Go on and enjoy yourself. I'll handle everything here. Heck, maybe I'll get it done faster with less distractions."

Margaret smiled. "Alright, Mom. Count me in. What time?"

Judy looked at her watch. "We're meeting at the Crescent Banquet Hall at four thirty so we can get settled in before bingo starts at five. Why don't you call Sarah and Donna and see if they want to come too."

"I'll do that now, but with their busy lives, who knows. They may be working. I'll see you then, Mom," Margaret said as she hung up.

* * *

Hours later, Margaret walked into the banquet hall right at 5 p.m., picked up her ticket and bingo cards, and scanned the noisy room full of folding tables, chairs, and women, trying to find her group.

"Over here!" Liz yelled and waved from across the room.

Margaret smiled as she maneuvered through the tight aisles until she got to their table where Judy, Audrey, Liz, Donna, and Sarah all sat sipping on wine and eating buffalo chicken dip and Hawaiian ham-and-cheese sliders.

"Hey, guys!" Margaret said as she squeezed into a chair next to Liz. "Sorry, I wasn't able to bring any goodies. I didn't have time to stop anywhere, and our kitchen is packed up."

Sarah scooped some dip on a chip. "Don't be sorry. We all understand."

Judy yelled from across the table. "What did you say, Margaret?"

Margaret yelled back over the very loud room. "I said I'm sorry I couldn't bring food or drinks!"

Judy shrugged, still having no clue what Margaret said, but Audrey filled her in.

Margaret looked to her right where some other women sat, noticing their many different colored ink blotters. "Oh, wow. You all came prepared."

The two women across from each other laughed. "You could say that. I even have sparkly ones in my purse," one of the women said as she pulled out five more ink blotters. "Did you need one?"

Margaret looked around the table, noticing everyone else came prepared. "I do actually. Could I borrow one? By the way, I'm Margaret, and this is Liz, Donna, Sarah, Audrey, and Judy."

Everyone nodded and said hello to each other.

"I'm Alice, and this is Connie," the woman said. "Feel free to take whatever ink blotter you want."

Margaret smiled and chose a sparkly green one, then looked at her bingo cards. "How do I do this? It's been forever."

Connie pulled tape out of her purse. "Here you go. Tape the bingo cards together on the sides. That way they're all together. It makes it easier. Trust me, we play bingo a lot."

Margaret laughed as she taped her bingo cards together. "You two are a riot. So, you really like doing these bingos, eh? Win anything good?"

Alice raised her hand. "I won three baskets of goodies and two purses at the bingo last weekend. We come way too often. I think our husbands are over it," she said with a laugh. "We're even going to Baltimore next weekend to do bingo."

Connie laughed. "We retired and became bingo fanatics. What happened to us?"

Just then, a guy they could barely see across the room got on the microphone, went over the rules, then started calling letters and numbers.

Five minutes later, after calling B6, a woman screamed *bingo* from across the room as her table of friends clapped and cheered.

Everyone else in the room moaned in disappointment that they didn't win and ripped off their bingo sheets ready to start anew.

The woman who won the high-end purse walked proudly back to her table and plopped the purse next to her, but then five people working the event surrounded the table and a commotion ensued. Next thing you know, one of the people working the event, took the purse, and walked it back to the front of the room where the other purses sat.

The woman stormed from the table, hollering, "That's my purse. I won it."

The worker shook their head. "You didn't have bingo. See, this is B5 not B6 on your card."

The woman stared at her card, trying to decipher if it really was B5 under all the ink, ultimately deciding it was as she slunk back into her seat and poured another glass of wine.

Margaret widened her eyes as she stared at the spectacle while Alice and Connie just shook their heads and chuckled.

"Have you seen this happen before?" Margaret asked the pair.

Alice raised her hand and laughed. "Drama at bingo? You bet. Grab the popcorn, because I'm sure more is coming."

Margaret glanced across the table at Judy while laughing. "Mom, what did you get me involved with here?"

Judy shrugged as she took a bite of her slider. "It's fun for everyone. Take a load off."

The guy on the microphone was back to calling numbers

again, and after twenty minutes of playing, Donna screamed, startling the whole table. "Bingo! Bingo! Bingo!"

Margaret grabbed her bingo card. "Did you check to make sure the numbers are right?"

Donna studied her card while looking at the numbers posted on the board on the wall. "Yep, all there," she said as she went up to collect her prize.

Donna walked back with her bright-red designer purse, smiling ear to ear, just as intermission was announced. She plopped it on the table for everyone to see. "Well, it will at least match my lobster sunburn from working on the boardwalk," she said with a chuckle.

Sarah propped her chin in her hands. "That's right. How's the funnel cake stand going? Are you glad you did it?"

Donna laughed. "Well, it's been an interesting few weekends to say the least."

"What do you mean?" Liz asked as she scooped up the buffalo chicken dip on a corn chip.

"Well, the air conditioner died twice. First, because it was old. Then, because someone plugged into my dedicated power on the boardwalk. My staff is great, but it hasn't exactly been the easy gig by the ocean that I'd pictured," she said with a chuckle.

Sarah nodded in agreement. "I concur. As you know, I've been helping Chris out with the birding boat since I have more free time now that I hired managers for the Monarch. I was so excited to be out on the water and working alongside him, but it's been one thing after another. I got really seasick at one point."

Liz's eyes widened. "No way. You? Seasick? I thought you loved being out on the boat?"

Sarah shrugged. "I do. This is the first time in my life that I've been seasick. I think it was a mix of what I ate and the big wake some other boats kicked up around us."

Audrey chimed in. "I totally get it. I've been seasick before. It's terrible."

Liz stretched her arms behind her head. "Mom, how's everything over at your place?"

Judy smiled as she took a sip of wine. "Well, it's great. Audrey and her family have been with us for a bit, and tomorrow is the big move-in day for everyone," she said with a smile as she glanced at Audrey and Margaret.

Liz nodded. "That's right. How's Dad? I haven't heard much from him lately."

Judy laughed. "He's been putting together everything he needs for a drive-in theater."

"A what?" Margaret asked, surprised.

"You heard right. We went to Wesley's Drive-in last month, and your father wanted to recreate it in the backyard. When he gets his mind fixated on something, there's no stopping him," Judy said with a chuckle. "Anyway, you're moving to your new home tomorrow. Are you excited?"

Margaret thought for a moment. "We *are* very excited, I guess I'm getting a little sentimental all of a sudden though. I'm sure it will pass, knowing that it will be in good hands," Margaret said as she glanced at Audrey.

"That's right, and we can't wait to move in," Audrey said.

Liz cut in. "Well, Greg thanks you, Margaret, for giving him all those winter sown plants. They're doing amazing in the garden he says."

Margaret smiled. "Good, I'm glad. There wasn't enough time to plant them at our new place. At least I got that experience in for next time. Has Greg finally put you to work out in the garden?"

Liz laughed. "I threw some flower seeds down recently. That's about it. I haven't had much interest since getting terrorized by mud, water, and bugs that one time."

Margaret rolled her eyes and chuckled. "I think you'll learn to love it."

* * *

Later that evening, Margaret got home from bingo to a fully packed house with moving boxes and disassembled furniture everywhere. It was quite the maze, but there in the middle of all the boxes in the living room was a family-style tent setup.

"Hello?" Margaret asked confused as she looked around the quiet house. "I'm home. Where is everyone?"

The girls poked their heads out of the tent. "We're in here."

"What are you two sillies doing?" Margaret asked as she walked over and looked inside the tent, noticing sleeping bags, a lantern, pillows, and books.

"Dave set this up for all of us. We're having a campout tonight," Harper said as she propped her elbow on her pillow and opened her book.

Dave came up from the basement holding an armload of comforters. "Oh, you're home!"

"I am," Margaret said as she took some blankets from him. "This is a nice tent you got set up here. I'm guessing these blankets go inside?"

Dave laughed. "They do. What do you think?"

Margaret laid the blankets out in the tent as the girls got up to help, then they plopped back down to read. "I love it. I'm assuming the girls will be spending the night in here?"

Abby poked her head out of the tent. "We're all sleeping in here."

Margaret glanced at Dave, who sheepishly shrugged.

"Everything is packed, and the mattresses are stripped. I figured it would be fun to have our last hurrah as a campout in the living room. What do you think?" Dave asked.

Margaret smiled as she got inside the tent. "Well, I think we'll make the most of it, but is anyone hungry? I ate some dip and a slider hours ago, but I'm starving, and we've got a big day tomorrow."

Just then, a light knock came from the back door.

Dave furrowed his brow in confusion. "Who is that? Nobody ever knocks on our back door."

Margaret's eyes widened. "Can you check?"

Dave walked over to the door and opened it. "Hey, guys! What's going on?"

Margaret and the girls got out of the tent to see what was going on. "Oh, my gosh! What's up guys?" Margaret said when she saw Liz, Greg, and their boys, Steven and Michael.

Liz ducked around some boxes, holding three boxes of pizza. "We wanted to stop by and see the place one more time. It was a spur-of-the-moment decision."

Greg grabbed the pizzas from Liz and put them on a clear spot on the counter, then took paper plates and napkins out of the bag Steven was holding. "Thought you all might like some pizza, so we stopped and picked up some pies."

Dave chuckled as he looked around the house, noticing nothing to sit on, as the kitchen chairs were stacked behind boxes and the couch and other chairs had boxes and other items piled on top of them to make room to walk. "Well, anyone up for sitting on the floor while we eat?"

Everyone took a slice and sat on the kitchen floor, making a circle facing each other.

Margaret took a bite of a Margherita slice and sighed. "This is so good. Thank you for bringing this, guys."

Greg and Dave started talking off to the side as well as Harper and Abby with Steven and Michael.

Liz smiled as she took a bite, then glanced at Margaret. "You talked about being sentimental about moving at bingo tonight, and I suddenly realized I was sentimental about it too. We were raised here, then you raised your daughters here. I know the house is staying in the family, but it won't be the same as my sister living here. I just needed to come back to have the final goodbye I think."

Margaret's eyes watered. "My gosh, I've been so excited

about moving that I don't think I took the time to have my goodbye with this house now that you mention it. I could name so many memories we've made here." She pointed to a corner of the kitchen. "Remember when you ran into the wall and chipped your tooth?"

Liz laughed. "How could I forget? I'd never seen Mom freak out like that. How about over there in the living room when Mom caught you on the couch kissing Dylan Humphreys?"

Dave's ears perked up, overhearing the conversation, and he laughed. "That's right. I remember Margaret saying she was a little bit wild in high school."

Margaret turned red with embarrassment while laughing. "It wasn't my proudest moment. I thought Mom was going to kill me."

Liz put her pizza down on the plate, working hard to contain her laughter.

Margaret took a deep breath with watery eyes and looked around the house. "I think this is the perfect way to have my goodbye with the house with you guys here. It just feels right."

CHAPTER TEN

Margaret waited outside, impatiently looking at her watch. "Where are they? They were supposed to be here two hours ago."

Dave walked outside and stood next to Margaret in the driveway, squinting into the sun. "Anything?"

Margaret shook her head. "Nobody picked up the phone. I can't get ahold of anyone. Not the cell phone number they gave me or the office."

Dave sighed and shook his head. "What is the deal with this moving company? It's not like they're running late with another move, we're the first move of the day—their 8 a.m. appointment."

Margaret shrugged. "I guess we'll just wait here. What else can we do? Though, Audrey and Rob are expected to start moving in this afternoon. I figured we'd be long moved out by then when we scheduled this."

Dave shook his head as he walked towards the backyard to let off some steam and do some thinking. When sounds of multiple vehicles could be heard coming into the driveway, he turned around with relief, figuring the moving company had finally arrived.

He crinkled his nose as he started walking back towards Margaret. "Is that the moving company?"

Margaret chuckled. "It's our friends."

Dave bit his lip. "Were they helping with the move today and I didn't know about it?"

Margaret waved at Chris and Sarah in their truck. "Not that I know of. This is as much of a surprise to me as it is you."

Donna and Dale, Liz and Greg, and Chris and Sarah all stepped out of their trucks and cars.

"Hey, guys," Margaret said. "What are you doing here?"

Liz smiled as she looked around. "I put together a little surprise help-out-with-Margaret-and-Dave's-move party, but where are the moving trucks?" she asked, confused.

Dave laughed. "They were supposed to have been here over two hours ago. We haven't heard a peep from them."

Just then, Rob and Audrey pulled onto their street in their moving truck.

As they approached, Margaret frowned. "Guys, I'm so sorry. We haven't moved a thing yet. Our moving company is two hours late."

Dave chimed in. "Who knows if they're even coming."

Audrey smiled and nudged Rob. "Oh, we know. Your parents told us after you called them this morning. We rented this extra moving truck for tomorrow for the new couch and dining room set we're picking up and decided to see if it would be of use to you all."

Dave gave a sigh of relief. "Thank you so much, guys. I think this moving company is not coming. We'll take all the help we can get."

Everyone rearranged their cars and trucks so Rob could back the moving truck into the driveway close to the house, then got to work hauling furniture, boxes, and even all of the outdoor supplies like bird baths, pots, gardening tools, and garden benches.

Two hours went by in the blink of an eye, and Rob pulled

down the back door of the moving truck, Chris strapped in the last dining room chair in the back of his truck's bed, and Liz and Donna squeezed in the last boxes into their cars.

Margaret handed out bottles of water to everyone and they all stood in a circle catching their breath and hydrating. Suddenly, Margaret's phone rang.

"Hello?" Margaret asked, not recognizing the number.

"Is this Margaret?"

"Yes, who is this?" Margaret asked.

"This is AJ from AJ's Movers calling you back. I got your message. You said you had us scheduled to come out this morning?"

Margaret nodded. "That's right. We've been waiting for hours."

AJ sighed and shook his head as he looked at his calendar. "I'm so sorry. My assistant must have put the date in wrong. We have you scheduled for tomorrow. My guys are already booked out on jobs today. Did you still want us to come tomorrow?"

Margaret looked at her friends and family as they stood around talking and the packed trucks and vehicles behind them. "No, I think we're good. Friends and family came through for us. We had to be out today."

AJ nodded. "Again, I'm so sorry. We can give you a discount on your next move."

Margaret laughed. "I don't think we plan to move again for a long while but thank you." She looked over at Audrey and Rob, then an idea sparked in her head. "You said that you still have your schedule open tomorrow morning? Can I get that discount for my cousin who's moving into our old house?"

AJ thought for a moment. "So, same location?"

Margaret nodded. "Yep. We hired you to move out, but instead I'm thinking your guys can help my cousin move into here. They don't even need a moving truck as they already have one packed. We'll tip them good, don't worry."

AJ nodded. "So, you don't need our moving truck, just help unloading into the house?"

"That's correct," Margaret said.

"Well, they'll get that done in less than an hour. My guys are fast movers. I'll tell you what, I'll give you half off for the inconvenience. My guys work by the hour, and I'm sure they'll only take an hour. It won't be much at all. Sound good?" AJ asked.

Margaret covered the speaker of her phone. "Audrey and Rob. Our moving company had us down for tomorrow. They're willing to make up for it by helping you guys unload tomorrow. Would that be OK?"

Rob nodded excitedly. "Yes, that would be amazing."

Dave looked at Margaret confused. "They had us down for tomorrow?"

Margaret rolled her eyes. "They put the date in wrong. We'll talk later." She uncovered the phone's speaker. "AJ? It's a deal. I'll handle the payment, so let the guys know."

"You got it," AJ said, feeling happy that everything had worked out. "And in the meantime, I'll get a better schedule system down so this doesn't happen again."

Margaret hung up and put the phone in her pocket. "Well, that worked out well. Is everyone ready to head over to the house?"

Moments later, Margaret and Dave's old home was in the rearview mirror as they drove away.

* * *

Dave and Margaret were the first in their caravan to drive up their new home's long gravel driveway. Margaret stared in awe at the purple, pink, and blue hydrangeas that lined the drive as they slowly made their way up.

"What? How did we not see this?" Margaret asked with widened eyes as she rolled down her window.

Dave smiled as he looked out his side of the window at the beautiful blooms. "Well, that final walkthrough was a week ago and in the evening. Maybe they hadn't bloomed yet, and the foliage was kind of hidden by the boxwoods in front of them."

Margaret nodded. "That explains it, but can you believe this? Hydrangeas all along our driveway. I'm even more in love."

When they got to the top of the driveway where the house sat, Margaret was again astonished to find blue hydrangeas bordering the entire front of the house. Everyone stepped out of their trucks and cars after parking, and looked around in awe, having never seen the property before except in photos.

Audrey scanned the area, then smiled. "I mean … we love your old house, Margaret, and we can't wait to move in tomorrow, but this is a major upgrade for you. This property is insane!"

Donna looked out towards the big meadow on the right side of the house. "It sure is. Is this all yours?"

Dave chuckled. "Yep. All ours. My weekends are going to be busy with all the mowing."

Margaret nudged Dave playfully, then looked towards the house. "Do you guys want to see the inside before we move everything in?"

Everyone nodded as they all followed Margaret towards the front door.

Margaret fiddled with her key chain, trying to find the right key. "It's on here somewhere."

Dave walked up next to Margaret. "Doing OK there?"

Margaret tried a key in the lock, but it wasn't the right key. "Not really. I thought I put the house key on my key chain, but none of these are right."

Dave grabbed her key chain. "Let me have a look," he said as he studied each one. "No, none of these are it. It was labeled with a white sticker."

Margaret put her head in her hands. "This is unbelievable. Do you have a copy?"

Dave shook his head. "Nope. Danielle only gave us the one key."

Margaret took out her phone. "Maybe she has an extra copy. I'm calling her."

Everyone else stood around talking as Margaret and Dave tried to quickly find a key to the house.

"Danielle!" Margaret yelled into her phone. "How ya doin'?"

Danielle smiled as she took a sip of her piña colada on the Florida beach she was laying out on. "I'm doing good. Hopped on a plane right after I saw you all. How's the new house?"

Margaret sighed. "Danielle, I'm going to get right to the point. We can't find our copy of the key you gave us."

Danielle laughed. "Well, I knew this was going to happen."

"What?" Margaret asked, confused.

Danielle nodded. "I've sold many houses, and I can't tell you how many times people lose their keys during moving-day madness. I made an extra copy. It's under the big rock on the right side of the house. I started doing that after my fifth client lost their key."

Margaret gave a sigh of relief and said, "Danielle, you're the best. We're going to go get it now," then turned to Dave and continued, "The key is under a large rock on the side of the house."

Danielle smiled. "Anytime. Call me if you need anything else or have any questions. I know moving into a new home isn't always easy."

"You're telling me. It's been an interesting day to say the least," Margaret said with a chuckle as Dave opened the front door with the newly found key.

Margaret said her goodbyes to their realtor and led everyone into the empty house. Every noise and voice echoed off the walls, but that didn't take away from the simplistic vintage beauty of the home.

Liz's eyes widened as she walked from room to room, taking mental notes of everything. She stopped in the sunroom and took a deep breath as everyone else toured different areas of the home.

"Margaret!" Liz called out as she walked to the living room fireplace and kneeled down to get a better view of it.

"Yeah?" Margaret asked from the kitchen where she was giving Donna, Dale, Audrey, and Rob a tour.

"Oh, sorry. I didn't realize you were in the kitchen," Liz said as she walked towards her.

"What's up?" Margaret asked.

Liz rubbed her hands together. "This house is amazing. Way better than any of the pictures I saw. There's so much potential," she said as she looked out the kitchen window towards the massive lush green property.

Greg popped into the kitchen with Dave, Sarah, and Chris. "I'm loving this kitchen. It has that old rustic farmhouse feel," Greg said.

Liz sighed. "Greg, I'm jealous. Can we move again? Can we find a home like this?"

Greg raised his eyebrows and shook his head. "We love our home. I'm not looking to sell it, well, ever."

Dave nodded. "Agreed. You've got a great place, Liz. Heck, I should know."

Just then, Judy and Bob, walked through the front door with Harper, Abby, Steven, and Michael in tow. "Hello, everyone! Are we late?" Judy asked.

Harper and Abby immediately ran upstairs to show off their empty bedrooms to the boys.

"We're just getting started, Mom," Margaret yelled towards the front door. "We're in the kitchen."

Bob walked into the room and set down a huge bag of

gummy bears. "Just in case anyone gets hungry," he said with a chuckle.

Dave held out his hand for a handshake with Bob. "Thanks for watching the kids and the cats. This morning was a fiasco with the moving company not showing up, but it worked out in the end."

"I see that it has," Bob said with a smile.

Chris cracked his knuckles. "Alright, we ready to start loading in?"

Dave nodded as the group followed him outside to the moving truck and vehicles.

"Let's start with the sectional," Dave said as he climbed into the back of the moving truck and raised the back sliding door.

Chris hoisted himself into the truck and started edging the couch out with the help of Dave and Dale. They managed to get the large couch off the truck and all the way to the front door, but that was it.

Dave stood in the doorway trying to pull the couch through. "The couch is too wide. Maybe if we spin it around," he said as more people came over to help position it better.

Dave tried to pull the couch through the doorway again, but it wasn't going to work.

"What about the back door?" Rob asked.

Dave nodded and wiped some sweat from his brow. "Let's try that," he said as Dale, Chris, and Rob led the way.

Meanwhile, everyone else hauled boxes and smaller items in through the front door and put them in whatever room was labeled on the box.

Dave got to the back door, swung it open, and attempted to pull the couch through again. "It's working. I've got it," Dave said.

They got the couch halfway through the doorway when it abruptly stopped moving.

"What in the world?" Dave asked as he looked around to see what the issue was.

Dale pointed behind Dave. "Look behind you. It's hitting that corner of the wall."

Dave sighed. "Well, the couch doesn't bend. How am I going to get it past the wall?"

Margaret and Liz set down the boxes they had just brought in and walked over to Dave, who was the only one inside the house holding the couch as the rest of the guys stood outside.

Liz scratched her chin. "Bring the couch back outside."

Greg shook his head. "Liz, not now. We've got a handle on this."

Margaret laughed. "It doesn't seem that way, guys."

Liz chimed in. "I can't tell you how many times I've finagled couches into difficult spots during my time as an interior designer. *Many* times. Trust me."

Dave sighed and motioned to the guys outside to back it up.

Liz looked at Margaret and smirked. "Let's do our magic, sister."

"OK, fellas, this is what we're going to do," Liz said as she stepped outside and motioned to the back door. "Dale is going to take that end, and Chris that end; Dave and Rob will get the middle. Margaret will stay inside to grab the front end with me. Flip the couch upside down, move it through doorway, and when I say *turn*, you're going to turn the couch slightly to the left? Got it?" Liz asked as she stepped back inside the house.

Greg chuckled. "OK, hon. We've got it."

"Great. OK, now start pushing the couch through," Liz said as she stood next to Margaret with her hands underneath the couch.

The guys pushed the couch through until Liz yelled, "Turn," and then the couch was turned to the left and pushed all the way through the doorway into the kitchen.

"We did it!" Margaret yelled as she high-fived Liz, then the guys.

Greg nodded, feeling impressed as the rest of the guys took a breather and wiped the sweat off their foreheads, relieved to finally have the couch in the house. "You did good, Liz. Now I know who to bring along when I'm helping my buddies move."

"Aw, shucks," Liz said as she nudged Greg.

CHAPTER ELEVEN

Chris walked out of the dock shop, then glanced out at the water and the sunrise. The rays illuminated everything they touched. It was quite spectacular. He looked around for Brewster, who usually rubbed his ankles whenever Chris had a moment to stand still, but then he remembered the feline had retired and was officially a house cat. Chris was sure he was most likely sunbathing in a window somewhere with a full belly and outstretched legs.

"I'm ready, boss," a voice came from behind Chris.

He whipped around to see Sarah up bright and early with white striped socks pulled up to her knees, cargo shorts held up by a belt, a green ribbed tank top, a baseball cap with a blue heron stitched on the front, and her brown hair cascading down onto her shoulders. Binoculars hung from her neck, and in her hand was the birding book she had been reading.

"Look at you," Chris said with a smile.

Sarah nodded, feeling fully confident. "I figured I'd dress the part today. I've been studying this book, and I'm ready to educate people on the boat about all those shorebirds."

Chris felt his heart skip a beat. "I thought after that seasick day that you were done. I'm surprised to see you to be honest."

Sarah put her binoculars up to her eyes and looked out onto the water, spotting an osprey out in the distance. "I almost threw in the towel, but I realized my limits. I can't eat right before getting on the boat. Problem solved."

Chris looked over Sarah's head as the customers for the first tour of the day arrived. "Well, it looks like we can start escorting everyone aboard."

Sarah playfully punched Chris's shoulder. "Let's do this, captain."

After getting everyone situated on the birding boat and going over the tips and rules, Chris started up the boat, and without hesitation, Sarah hopped onto the dock to untie the boat before getting back on.

"All good, captain," Sarah said from the deck as she smiled at Chris. Then she turned around to point birds out to the people around her.

Chris guided the boat to a secluded spot surrounded by marshes, then cut the engine. The pontoon boat bobbed gently as everyone looked out the windows or made their way out onto the deck to get a better look.

Chris scanned for birds with his binoculars when Sarah screamed out, "There's a blue heron fishing at six o'clock."

Chris nodded and chuckled as he got a glimpse of the shorebird Sarah pointed out. "Yep, there he is. Does everyone see it?"

The customers nodded, affirming their answers by watching in anticipation to see if the heron would catch it's intended meal. Sure enough, the blue heron walked slowly through the marsh, then suddenly stopped and cocked its head. A moment later, it thrust its beak into the water, pulled out a speared fish, flipped it up, and swallowed it whole. The tour group was amazed to see it.

Before Chris got a word out, Sarah pointed off to the right. "We've got some oystercatchers at one o'clock, folks. They've got that long orange-red bill that's used for prying open mollusks and other such food."

Chris quietly looked through his binoculars, feeling happy that the love of his life was suddenly into birding as much as he was. He let her do all the talking with the customers, then started up the boat again.

"Alright, everyone. We're going to head to another good location. I think we'll find a lot to look at over there," Chris said as Sarah walked up and stood next to him, adjusting her baseball cap.

"I packed us lunches for afterwards. I figured we could sit at the picnic table on the dock and watch the boats go by," Sarah said as she looked up at him with a smile.

Chris glanced at her. "You've outdone yourself today. I think you've officially got your sea legs. I'm proud of you. I can't wait to eat lunch together on this beautiful day."

* * *

Margaret was upstairs in their bedroom unpacking a bin full to the brim with clothing and putting it into the dresser.

Dave poked his head into the doorway. "Hey. How's it going up here?"

Margaret smiled and sighed, feeling happy but exhausted. "It's going. I forgot how tiring moving is. We've been at this for hours."

Dave nodded. "I'm glad your parents have the girls and the cats this week. It at least gives us time to get a little settled. I just unpacked most of the kitchen, and I'm going to go start hanging the bamboo blinds and curtains in the living room."

Margaret put the last piece of folded clothing into the drawer and pushed it closed. "I'll come and help you. I think this room is mostly done."

Dave led the way downstairs before stopping at the bottom of the stairwell and stared at the wall. "Thankfully, this place was move-in ready, but we'll have to pick out some colors that suit us better, and I have lots of projects in mind."

Margaret walked into the living room and picked up a blind. "I'm glad we got escrow to close so quickly. It will be exciting to make this place our own after we've gotten all moved in."

After another few hours of unpacking and hanging curtains and blinds, Dave sat on the hardwood floor and leaned against the wall while taking a long drink of water from his bottle. Margaret did the same from the across the room, while holding her shirt away from her body to cool off.

"It's a shame this place doesn't have central air. I can't believe we got all of this done with just a few fans," Margaret said, feeling hot, dirty, and tired.

Dave took another long sip of his water, then looked around. "We'll have to go get some air-conditioning units for the windows. July is around the corner, and then it's going to be really hot."

Margaret fanned her face. "I can't believe we moved from a house with central air to one without in the summer. Are we crazy?"

Dave laughed and hopped up to his feet. "We've been working all morning and afternoon. Let's go outside and take a breather. We haven't walked around the property since it's officially become ours. What do you say?" Dave asked as he helped Margaret up with one hand.

Margaret brushed herself off, then opened the front door. "Outside it is!"

They stood out on the porch together, admiring the blue hydrangeas before walking out towards the meadow.

Margaret stopped in the middle of the meadow and pointed at the soil. "Right here is where I want my cut flower bed someday."

Dave thought for a moment. "I bet we still have time to

plant some fast-producing flower seeds. Zinnias and marigolds for sure. Probably some sunflowers too."

"You think?" Margaret asked, surprised. "We have so much work to get done on the house. Shouldn't that be priority?"

Dave nodded. "The house is definitely the priority, but we'll make some extra time for the yard. I know it's important to you."

"That would be amazing. Maybe we can get in a little herb garden too over by the back door," Margaret said.

Dave scratched his head. "You know? When I was growing up on the farm, we did plant extra vegetables at the end of June like cucumbers, beans, pumpkins, summer and winter squash … actually there was a lot of stuff. I think we can still get a garden in."

Margaret squealed in delight. "That's music to my ears. I'm so happy you're on board with this."

Dave put his arm around Margaret's neck and pulled her close. "I definitely am, but I'm also on board with filling our tummies with food. Let's go grab something to eat."

"You read my mind. How about tacos?" Margaret asked as they walked together back to the house.

"Now you read *my* mind," Dave said.

Forty minutes later, they found themselves sitting outside of Key West Tacos, eating their scrumptious meal.

Dave's eyes rolled back in his head as he took a bite. "Amazing. This hits the spot."

"Mm-hmm," Margaret agreed happily as she took a bite of hers.

Dave swallowed and wiped his mouth. "Tomorrow."

"Tomorrow what?" Margaret asked.

"I'm going to get the garden plots ready tomorrow. We can't wait much longer. It's going to be July in a little over a week," Dave said as he took another bite of his taco.

"Seriously?" Margaret asked, surprised. "We have a million

things to do in the house, though. The garden shouldn't be at the top of the list."

Dave shook his head. "We'll get it all done. Don't worry. I'll get up extra early."

Margaret smiled as she took her last bite, then took a long sip of her drink. "Ok, then, Mr., We'll get caffeinated up and go to town tomorrow. I can't wait."

* * *

Dale walked around his dimly lit market restaurant, lighting tea light candles on the tables and ledges. It was a warm night, so the front pull-up garage doors were wide open, letting in a nice summer breeze.

A knock came from the outside, and in walked Greg holding a crate of zucchini. "Hey, Dale. Just dropping off this squash we grew for the market. We have more than we know what to do with."

Dale grabbed the crate from Greg and placed it on the front counter. "Thanks, man. I appreciate it."

Greg nodded as he glanced around the beautiful space Dale had made with his crew. "This is incredible, Dale. It's such a unique idea for a restaurant. I think it's going to do really well."

Dale smiled and sighed as he walked over to a few more candles and lit them. "I sure hope so. I really want this to work out so I can live and work in Cape May. You did it right, Greg. Your restaurant is a success, even only open four days a week, and you're close to home. I'm trying to follow in your footsteps."

Greg ran his hands through his hair. "Aw, shucks. Well thanks, Dale. I appreciate that. So, opening day is tomorrow?"

"It sure is," Dale said as the timer went off in the kitchen.

"Well, I won't keep you. Looks like a little something special is going on in here tonight," Greg said with a smile.

Dale headed back to the kitchen. "I'm treating Donna to dinner, just the two of us, before the grand opening. I've got everything cooking, and I have to finish the starter salad."

"Hi, guys," Donna said as she walked inside.

Greg said his hellos and goodbyes and quickly made his way to his car while Dale worked feverishly in the kitchen adding feta cheese, croutons, kalamata olives, red onion, and tomatoes to the spring mix salad. He tossed it with a red wine vinaigrette and popped the fresh-baked bread out of the oven.

"Hey, you," Dale said as he walked to a candlelit table with a vase holding a dozen red roses placed in the center of it. "Are you hungry?"

Donna set down her purse and took seat, pouring the white wine that was sitting in a bucket of ice next to the table into the two wine glasses. "I'm completely hungry, and also completely blown away by this place, Dale. How am I only seeing it now?"

Dale placed the salads, fresh bread, and butter on the table and took a seat next to Donna. "Well, I wanted you to see it finished. A grand reveal. It's just something I wanted to do."

Donna chuckled as she took a sip of wine then took a bite of the salad. "Oh, this salad. You're making me this at home. I'd eat this every day."

"I knew you'd like it," Dale said as he took a bite of his crusty warm bread.

Twenty-five minutes of conversation later, Dale's alarm went off in the kitchen. "I'll be right back," he said as he jumped up and ran to the kitchen to take the food out of the oven. He plated the roasted chicken breast with the crisp balsamic brussels sprouts and cheesy potatoes, then brought them out to the table.

Donna's eyes lit up. "My gosh, Dale. You went to so much trouble for this dinner. So sweet of you," she said as she stared at how beautifully the food was presented.

"I try," Dale said with a smile. Just as he was about to take a bite, he remembered something. "Did you happen to see the name of the restaurant?"

Donna thought for a moment. "No, I didn't notice out front, and I'm realizing that you've never told me. What is it?"

Dale stood up and held his hand out for Donna. "Let's go outside before the food gets cold so you can see."

Donna shrugged, stood up and walked outside to the charmingly lit large wooden sign above the restaurant. She squinted her eyes to make sure she was seeing correctly. "Does that say Donna's?"

Dale nodded and grabbed her hand and kissed it. "It does. It took me some time to come up with a name, and I finally realized the perfect name for this restaurant because you are the reason I love being in Cape May. You're the reason I wanted to work here. You're the reason I wanted to start fresh so I could have more time for a life ... with you. It only seemed fitting to name it after you."

Tears formed in Donna's eyes as she wrapped her arms around Dale and buried her head in his chest. "Dale, this is the nicest thing anyone has ever done for me."

Dale rubbed her back and kissed her head as he stared up at the sign, feeling in that moment that everything was working out as it should.

Donna wiped the tears from her eyes, then started back to the table. "We'd better eat this wonderful meal, Dale. We'll have many more days to stand in front of the sign and hug."

Dale took one last moment outside with himself, staring at the restaurant under the sign and moonlight. He had never felt so in love with any place in his life as he did now in Cape May.

CHAPTER TWELVE

Donna was out early on Friday to open up the funnel cake stand. She looked over at Becky, who was opening the corn cart next door, smiled and nodded.

"It's going to be a hot one today," Donna said as she stocked the front window ledge with napkins and plastic utensils.

Becky chuckled. "Oh, don't I know it. I'm sure we'll be a sweaty mess after this."

Donna sighed as she looked across the boardwalk to the waterslides that were already flowing with people. "Say, what time are you done today?"

Becky looked at her watch. "Today's an early day for me. Around three. Someone's coming in for the next shift then."

Donna finished restocking the front of the cart and walked to Becky's window. "What do you say you and I go cool off on some waterslides after work? I'm also done around three. My employees are good enough to be on their own now, and I trust them."

Becky's eyes sparkled as she looked towards the slides and pools on the pier. "You know, I have been dying to get on that lazy river. This hot weather has me dreaming about floating in it for hours straight with my head back and eyes closed."

Donna clapped her hands. "Let's do it, then. I've got nothing going on. I could use some fun."

Becky smiled ear to ear, but then remembered. "I don't have a bathing suit though. It's at home."

Donna waved her hand in the air. "No problem. We'll go to one of the shops on the boardwalk and get one after we're done."

Becky shucked corn from inside the cart and nodded. "Sounds like we've got ourselves a plan."

Donna walked back to her cart and started making funnel cake batter when tons of people started getting in line. "Oh, wow. It's going to be a busy day," Donna said to herself as she dusted off her hands and peered out the front window to get the first person's order.

Just then, Olivia walked in, throwing an apron over her head and tying it around her waist. "I'm here. I'm here. Sorry. It was so hard to find parking. The boardwalk is insanely crowded."

Donna chuckled. "I can tell. Look at the line in front of the cart already."

Olivia's eyes widened. "This early? Funnel cake for breakfast it is, then," she said as she took cash from the customer and gave them their change while Donna scooped apple pie filling onto to the hot funnel cake.

By three o'clock, Donna and Olivia were peeling off their aprons, and Josh and Russ were arriving for their shift.

"Thanks, guys," Donna said as she got them situated with everything in the cart. "I'm warning you. It's going to be busy. Olivia and I didn't have a moment to breathe."

Olivia laughed. "That's right. I'm hitting the beach. I'll see you all later," she said as she picked up her beach chair that had been laying against the back of the cart.

Becky met Donna behind the funnel cake cart. "Let's go

get some bathing suits already. I need to get in the water now, and the longer I stay here, the longer I'm going to get sucked into helping out with the corn cart."

Twenty minutes later, and they were in their neon bikinis and white mesh cover-ups booking it down the boardwalk to the water slides while laughing. Donna looked down. "I can't believe we bought these bathing suits. They're hideous."

Becky laughed. "It's all they had. It sure isn't good for my pale complexion."

They got to the pier, paid for waterpark tickets, put their belongings in a locker and made their way to the lazy river.

Donna hopped into a big yellow tube and Becky did the same.

Becky splashed some cold water onto her body as they peacefully floated along, occasionally bumping into other's inner tubes. "So, how did today go?" Becky asked as she lifted her sunglasses to look at Donna.

Donna smiled. "Today was the best day yet. I counted out our register before Josh and Russ showed up, and I'm astonished at what a profit these carts can pull. Fifteen hundred dollars just for the first half of the day. I'm not sure I ever want to give this up."

Becky laughed. "We did pretty good too, but not that good. I have to say, I am really starting to love this gig. Maybe it can be our summer jobs when we finally become teachers."

Donna sighed as she tilted her head back and looked up at the sky. "Becky, I love being back in school, but I'm really starting to rethink this teaching career. I think I'm going to switch majors to business. I'm starting to realize that I love working for myself. I love running businesses."

Becky stared up at the sky with Donna and kicked her feet into the water. "I think you're onto something, Donna. Whatever it is, I'm glad I found you. You're inspiring me to get out there and do fun things like this again."

* * *

That afternoon, Margaret and Dave were working their butts off—unpacking, cleaning, and setting all of the rooms up with furniture.

Dave poured a huge glass of iced tea, then looked out the back kitchen window towards the yard. "Well, I think it's time. We got up early and got everything done inside the house. Let's tackle these gardens."

Margaret was more than ready. She walked down the stairs caring three huge craft bins full of seeds. "What was that?" she asked as she set the bins down on the kitchen counter.

Dave chuckled and shook his head. "You beat me to it. I was saying we need to get out in the yard now," he said as he opened the back door.

Margaret's face lit up as she snatched the bins off the counter and stepped outside, Dave closing the door behind them.

"Well, I'm going to grab the rototiller out of the garage," Dave said as he turned his hat backwards and walked away.

Margaret found a patch of grass and laid out her seeds, trying to figure out what she wanted to plant where.

Suddenly, she heard a loud engine roar to life from the garage, then Dave was moving towards her sitting atop a tractor and smiling ear to ear. "They left a tractor with a plow. Nice one too," Dave said as he hopped off and studied it.

Margaret crinkled her nose. "Did they mean to leave this? I don't think we should be using it."

"Oh, they meant it. There was a note attached to it. I think Danielle might have put it there for them," Dave said as he handed the piece of paper to Margaret.

To the buyers of our home, Margaret and Dave,

We picked you two because we knew you'd appreciate the beauty of the land like we did. My wife loved to garden, and it was one of her greatest joys when she could physically do it. Now, she tends to a handful of house-plants here in Florida, though it's up for debate how well they're doing. Anyway, we left a few surprises with the purchase of the house. One of them being this tractor. I plowed up many plots for my lovely wife to plant her flowers. I hope you can make some good use of it. Send us pictures if you can.

Henry Lewis

Margaret's heart leaped. "A tractor? Surprises? Is this a dream?" she asked as she handed the letter back to Dave.

Dave got back on the tractor and started it up. "I sure hope not," he said as he drove to a plot of land and started plowing the earth up.

Margaret filled her pockets with seeds packets and walked over to where Dave was plowing and watched, feeling thoroughly happy and inspired with how life was turning out.

"Hey, Dad," Margaret said joyfully when her phone rang from her pocket.

"Hello, my daughter. I've got a proposition for this evening," Bob said.

"Oh?" Margaret said, growing curious.

"Well, I've got everything for a functioning drive-in movie. I'd like to set it up tonight on your property. I know you guys are probably super busy, but would you be OK with taking some time out to have a special backyard viewing?" Bob asked optimistically.

Margaret chuckled. "Of course. Can we invite more friends and family?"

Bob smiled from ear to ear. "You sure can. Tell them to arrive by seven o'clock."

Margaret scratched her head. "It won't be dark until well past seven, though, Dad."

Bob shrugged. "There will be other stuff besides movies.

Tell them to come early. In the meantime, I'll be by in a bit to get set up."

"OK, Dad. Dave and I are making garden plots and planting seeds. Come find us if you need anything."

* * *

Meanwhile, Greg walked around his own lush garden, stopping to admire the flower patch that Liz had planted. Nothing had bloomed yet, as it had only been a few weeks, but the plants were vibrant and full.

Liz walked outside, holding her phone to her cheek. "Greg! Margaret and Dave invited us over for some kind of drive-in that Dad is putting on tonight."

Greg crinkled his nose. "Drive-in?"

Liz nodded. "Yeah, I guess it's supposed to be his version of a drive-in theater. Anyway, it sounds like fun. We'll head over around six thirty if that works."

Greg nodded. "Sounds good. I'm sure the boys will love it."

Liz squinted her eyes, staring at the garden patch where she planted the flower seeds. "Is that what I planted? All of that?"

Greg smiled. "It is. Looks like we're going to get a ton of flowers over here."

Liz put the phone back up to her ear. "Sorry, Margaret. Yes, we'll be over. We'll bring some snacks. See you then." She hung up, then stood next to Greg, looking at the flower plot. "So, this is everything I planted? All of those seeds? They actually grew?" Liz asked, astonished as she eyed up all of the green growth.

"Yep! Can you believe it?" Greg said with a chuckle.

Liz clapped her hands and a did a hop. "I can't wait to see what they look like when they bloom. I'm going to make bouquets for the house and the restaurant, and maybe Mom and Dad will want some and—"

Greg laughed and put his hand on Liz's shoulder. "So, you want to help out in the garden now?"

Liz shrugged and smirked. "Maybe I'll get dirty once in a while," she said as she headed to the house. "I'm going to go whip something up for tonight. It's supposed to be a nice evening. I'm looking forward to it."

Greg paused and took in the property one last time before turning off the hose and putting the garden tools back in the garage. He understood why Margaret and Dave loved being out in the garden so much. The bug had bit him and perhaps Liz too.

* * *

Dave had finished plowing and was now helping Margaret broadcast the flower seeds in the rich soil.

"I'm running low. What else do you have for me?" Dave asked while holding out his hands to Margaret.

Margaret reached deep into her pocket. "I have one packet left of California Giant zinnia seeds. Have at 'em," she said while handing it over to him.

They spread the rest of the seeds, watered them in with the hoses, then stopped to take long sips of their fresh lime-and-mint seltzer drinks that Margaret had put together in the kitchen.

"Where's your dad?" Dave asked after he took another long sip.

Margaret shrugged. "I saw them pull in with the kids, but I haven't a clue. Maybe on the other side of the house."

Dave pulled the old owner's letter out of his pocket, forgetting that it was in there. He read it again, then looked out past the tree line. "I wonder what other surprises they're talking about. We already found the greenhouse, lighthouse, and rosebushes, which were pretty amazing."

Margaret bit her lip. "Let's go explore. We've got an hour

before everyone arrives. Maybe we'll find my parents and Harper and Abby in the meantime," she said as she took Dave's hand and led him toward the trees.

They walked farther this time, past the pond and the greenhouse and out to another meadow and back to another tree line.

"I don't know if this our property, Margaret," Dave said, feeling a little concerned.

Margaret shrugged. "I think it is. I looked at the map Danielle gave us, and it seemed like it went pretty far back."

Just then, they heard Bob and Judy talking loudly through the thick trees.

"Mom?! Dad?!" Margaret yelled out.

"We're over here," Judy yelled back.

Dave stood still, trying to figure out which direction their voices came from. "This way. They're back in that direction," Dave said as he led the way.

"Mom!" Margaret yelled again, louder.

"We're here, dear!" Judy yelled, this time sounding about fifty feet ahead of them.

Dave found a driveway dirt path between the trees, and they walked down it until they came to something right out of a book.

Margaret gasped when she saw where her parents and Abby and Harper were.

There, right under some tall oak trees was a thousand-square-foot patch of vibrant fluffy green grass bordered with hydrangeas in pink, blue, and purple, just like along the driveway. In the middle sat a large fountain. Behind the hydrangeas, was a gentle creek flowing with water, but that wasn't all. Bob had driven his baby-blue 1960 Chevy Impala convertible onto the grass and set up a large blow-up outdoor screen, complete with speakers.

"How do you like it?" Bob asked as he opened his arms towards the screen, showing off his work.

"Hi, Mom! Hi, Dave!" Abby and Harper both yelled in unison.

Dave was bewildered. "This is amazing, Bob. But how did you find this part of the property? We had no clue this even existed."

Bob shrugged. "We kept driving down dirt paths until we found a good patch of land. Judy spotted this area."

Judy nodded in agreement. "I also put out a table with snacks and drinks, and over there on the right, we have corn-hole and ladder ball set up for games."

"I'd better get back to the house and direct everyone where to go," Dave said as he started back.

Moments later, everyone arrived with Dave guiding the way to the secret hydrangea spot. They brought folding beach chairs, blankets, and snacks with them.

Donna opened her and Dale's chairs, then greeted Bob and Judy. "I heard you two did all of this. How fun!"

Judy pointed to Bob. "It was his idea. He got annoyed about the food situation at the drive-in theater we went to and wanted to recreate it. Margaret and Dave's big property seemed the perfect spot, especially to play the audio loud on the movie. We shouldn't disturb any neighbors all the way out here."

"What are we watching tonight, Mom and Dad?" Liz asked as she moseyed over with Steven and Michael.

"Well, we had to keep it family friendly, but *The Secret Garden* seemed fitting after hearing about the greenhouse—now it's even more fitting with this beautiful open space by the creek," Judy said with a smile.

Sarah and Chris walked to the snack stand and plated up some sandwiches, chips, and dips, before grabbing drinks and mingling with everyone else.

"I'm in love with your yard and property," Sarah said to Margaret and Dave as she took a bite of her sandwich.

Dave looked at Margaret and slipped his arm around her. "We are too, thank you."

Bob, who stood by the projector, cleared his throat loudly. "Everyone, take your seats. The movie is about to begin," he said as he got it up and running.

Judy got into the convertible along with Bob, and they cuddled up together, looking at the big screen through the windshield.

Meanwhile, Dave set up a blanket off to the side for himself, Margaret, and the girls, but the kids chose to go play games with their cousins.

Dave put his arm around Margaret as they sat on the blanket, watching the movie start. He turned his head to look around the perfect piece of land they owned, with its own secret garden that they didn't even know existed until now. "I don't think we could have found a more perfect place to build a life together."

Margaret leaned her head on his shoulder and gave a happy sigh. "I agree. There's enough land for everyone we love to build a home on it. We could set up a little village," she half-joked.

Dave laughed. "Let's focus on what we have now and work from there. There's so much that we could do here."

Margaret perked up. "I know. I have so many wild dreams about what I want to do with this land. But for now, let's take in the hydrangeas, the warm summer night, the sound of the stream next to us, and relish this moment so we'll remember it forever."

EPILOGUE

On a hot July day, Margaret was out in the garden wearing a wide-brim sun hat. She kneeled down to pinch off some suckers on the tomato plants they'd put in the ground last month. They were late to go in due to the move but were expected to still produce tomatoes into September.

Dave stood up from weeding around the cucumber and squash plants and looked over at Margaret through the tall, lush vegetable garden. "Not bad for starting a summer garden a month late, eh?" he said as he brushed his hands together to knock the dirt off.

Margaret sighed as the scorching sun beat down on them. "Not bad at all. I'm quite impressed with this, to be honest. Did you see the herb patch? It's massive."

Dave looked towards the house where Abby and Harper played on the swing set that he'd installed the day prior. "I think working weekends, mornings, and nights on the house has really paid off. We got the walls painted, shelves installed, and new tile in the bathrooms. There's still a lot to do, but enough has been done that we can relax and enjoy it all."

Margaret tipped her hat up to look at Dave. "I'm definitely enjoying it all out here," she said with a smile.

Dave nodded and smiled, then picked up his garden tools and placed them on a nearby picnic table.

Margaret walked over to her large herb patch and reached down to pick some lavender, then put it up to her nose to smell it. She glanced at Dave. "You know, I've been thinking about how amazing all this land is. I want to be able to share it with others."

Dave took a long gulp of his fresh-brewed iced tea that Margaret had made with her herbs. "What do you mean?"

"Well, you know … there aren't enough tea houses in Cape May. I know the bed-and-breakfasts do tea hour, but a lot of times, you need to be a guest to partake. I have this grand idea of starting a tea garden. It would be reservation only, so it wouldn't be open all the time and I could work it out with my schedule, but what do you think?"

Dave thought for a moment, not sure of how he felt about the idea. "So, like a business?"

Margaret nodded. "Yes, but a side business. You know how full my schedule is between the Seahorse Inn and my job at Pinetree Wildlife Refuge. Then again, the Seahorse is running like a well-oiled machine without Liz and I being there very often. We've got some great ladies holding the fort down. Maybe I will have more time to focus on this?"

"Do you think it would turn a profit? Would it be worth your while?" Dave asked, still trying to determine if it was a good idea or not.

"I think so, and if it doesn't, then I'll close it. I think the hydrangea area back behind the house might be a perfect spot," Margaret said pointing to the tree line.

Dave scratched his chin. "Or … over in the shady area by the pond near the greenhouse?"

Margaret smiled. "You're right. That's also a good location. There're so many great choices on this property."

Dave gazed off into the distance, deep in thought. "I could

probably build some structures to help with this business idea. Maybe some pergolas over decking."

Margaret squealed with delight. "I could train grapevines to grow up them, and they would shade the tables and chairs underneath. I could even make a large butterfly garden and a cottage garden that the guests could walk through."

Dave nudged her playfully. "You sure can dream up things. What are you going to do for tea during the hot summer though?"

Margaret pointed to his mason jar full of fresh-brewed tea. "Iced tea, but there will also be other refreshing drinks like my blackberry honey water and lavender lemonade. I can leave the hot tea for spring and fall. My gosh, I'm getting more excited about this by the minute."

* * *

Pick up **Book 11** in the Cape May Series**, Cape May Sunshine,** to follow Margaret, Liz, the rest of the familiar bunch, and some new characters.

Follow my Facebook page at https://www.facebook.com/ClaudiaVanceBooks

ABOUT THE AUTHOR

Claudia Vance is a writer of women's fiction and clean romance. She writes feel good reads that take you to places you'd like to visit with characters you'd want to get to know.

She lives with her boyfriend and two cats in a charming small town in New Jersey, not too far from the beautiful beach town of Cape May. She worked behind the scenes on television shows and film sets for many years, and she's an avid gardener and nature lover.

Book cover design by Red Leaf Design

* * *

Made in the USA
Las Vegas, NV
16 May 2022